Twits on the Stump

A STEAMPUNK DISTRACTION

TOM ALAN ROBBINS

BOOK SEVEN OF THE TWITS CHRONICLES

Claim A Free Gift!

Visit Twitschronicles.com to claim a free copy of the Twits short story *Uncle Hugo's Crisis.* Or, if you are reading this on a device, you can click HERE.

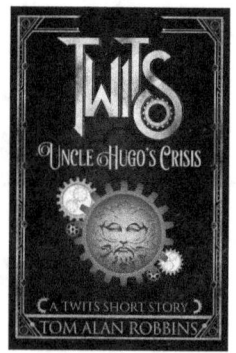

The Author makes no representation of any kind as to his being a citizen of the United Kingdom, either native or naturalized. He is from a small town in Ohio, for which he apologizes.

Copyright © 2023 by Tom Alan Robbins

Cover design by Melody J. Barber of Aurora Publicity

Additional designs by Eric Wright of The Puppet Kitchen.

Twits Logo designed by Feppa Rodriquez

Proofreading by Gretchen Tannert Douglas

What People Are Saying:

"The Twits Chronicles are hilarious, blessed with truly exceptional dialogue. Steampunk dystopia meets Oscar Wildean wit in these books. I found myself laughing out loud on numerous occasions--and that's not something I often do while reading. "

—Nick Sullivan, author of The Deep Series and Zombie Bigfoot.

"Delightful! A frothy frappe of P.G. Wodehouse and steam-punk. If you're the sort who reads blurbs before reading the book, stop it. Stop it right now. Read TWITS IN LOVE and have a good time. These days we can all use a bit more of a good time."

—John Ostrander, American writer of comic books, including *Suicide Squad, Grimjack* and *Star Wars: Legacy.*

"I haven't enjoyed the company of such eccentric characters since A Confederacy of Dunces, and Tom Alan Robbins has managed to place them in the stylized world of Oscar Wilde. A really unique journey."

— Kevin Conroy, Actor, The voice behind the DC Comics superhero Batman .

"Tom Alan Robbins' Twits stories are hilarious, thought provoking and mind bending. His juicy turns of phrase will stick in your ear like a catchy song."

— Michael Urie, Actor, Producer and Director

"Tom is the most talented, delicious writer. Do yourself a favor, and immerse yourself in the fabulous world of TWITS!"

— Mary Testa, 3 time Tony Award Nominee

For Lisa, Kevin, David and all the golden children of my youth who solved the mystery much too soon.

Steampunk

"Steampunk is a subgenre of science fiction that incorporates retrofuturistic technology and aesthetics inspired by 19th-century industrial steam-powered machinery. Steampunk works are often set in an alternative history of the Victorian era or the American "Wild West", where steam power remains in mainstream use, or in a fantasy world that similarly employs steam power."

Wikipedia

A Word About Timelines

For those who are unfamiliar with the Steampunk genre, a word about timelines may be helpful. The Steampunk Universe in which The Twits Chronicles take place is clearly not our own. That is why events and cultural references that happened in vastly different eras in our own world seem to happen in a compressed time period. It feels as if we are in a vaguely Victorian era, and yet there are references to events and quotations from well into the twentieth century.

It may help to think of this as an exercise in "what if?" What if electricity wasn't discovered until much later in human history? Human ingenuity would still search for new ways of using existing technology, and so steam power and mechanical engineering would keep advancing, while much of the aesthetic of the world around us could remain in the nineteenth century. The art of running a political campaign, with its attendant arts of misinformation and mass persuasion would also advance, alas.

The world that would result is the world of *The Twits Chronicles*. Other writers would use these same criteria to create very different realities. This is mine.

Enter and enjoy.

Contents

Preface

The Twits Chronicles, which currently stand at eight volumes, follows the adventures of Cyril Chippington-Smythe and his steam-powered valet, Bentley. I encourage readers to consume them in order—there is a certain amount of growth on Cyril's part as he navigates one perilous adventure after another. For anyone who is diving in at Book Eight, however, a *precis* may be useful.

The world of Twits is one devastated by climate change and economic inequality. This may seem a strange choice for comedy, but I believe in the dictum that "Comedy is tragedy plus time." We could not be farther away from the events in these books in terms of time, since they take place in an alternate reality where historical events have turned out very differently from our own.

Cyril and his friends and family are members of a privileged class. Indeed, he may be the richest man in the world. His ancestor discovered the secret of turning seawater into hydrogen, thus Cyril owns all of the world's hydrogen plants.

In this insulated world of incredible wealth and privilege, the inhabitants have nothing with which to occupy themselves but fashion, games of status, rituals of tribal identity and the frivolous pursuit of "love".

There is one thing standing between Cyril and this yawning, existential pit of meaningless existence—his brilliant, mechanical manservant, Bently. Built by a company that used to manufacture luxury automobiles, Bentley has been with the family for several generations. He practically raised Cyril, whose parents are mysteriously absent, and is always present to extricate Cyril from his predicaments. Through his tutelage, Cyril has actually begun to develop something approaching a conscience- a rare commodity among his class.

Hopefully you are up to speed now and ready to enter the world of *Twits Hit the Target*. Thank you for visiting.

CHAPTER ONE

The Problem with Pies

Loyal readers of these chronicles will have gleaned that I, Cyril Chippington-Smythe, believe "love" to be bunco. My nearest and dearest have fallen prey to it over the years and my response has been a haughty stare and a supercilious sniff. My cousin Binky (Cheswick Wickford-Davies to his creditors), however, falls in love as though buying in bulk earns him a discount.

On this particular Spring day, he was composing odious odes and setting them to atonal melodies in honour of a young lady he had met at a pie shop. He was purchasing a porky pie and she was agitating for the rights of those who produced said pies.

Binky and I were lolling about in my richly appointed bedroom. I had gotten in the habit of staying in bed for most of the morning, sipping tea and munching on whatever Cook was inspired to bake. I was beginning to notice a small protuberance in my midsection, but the girdle took care of that. Bentley, my steam-powered valet, was gliding here and there keeping order and refilling teacups when necessary.

"What rhymes with Forsythia?"

I thought for a moment. "Galicia, if you pronounce it as they do in Santiago de Compostela."

He mumbled to himself for a moment and shook his head. "Too geographical."

"Arrythmia is rhyme adjacent."

He hummed something that sounded like a hive of mechanical bees in distress and sang in a kind of moan, "Show me some pity, my darling Forsythia. You cause my heart to experience arrythmia."

"I beg you to stop."

"Wasn't there someone Greek named Pythia?"

Bentley cleared his throat. Bentley's mechanical brain is a miracle of technology and I have yet to see him stumped when information is required.

"That was the name given to one of the High Priestesses of ancient Greece, Sir. She was also known as the Oracle of Delphi."

Binky concentrated fiercely. "A song for the beautiful goddess Forsythia. You lay bare my future like the priestess called Pythia."

I groped about in the bedclothes until I found a slipper which I hurled at his head.

"One more rhyme and I shall have Bentley throw you down the stairs. No woman is worth it."

"You must meet her, Cyril. She is an angel."

"I've lost count of the number of angels you've introduced me to whose wings turned out to be made of sticks and muslin. Let me know when you meet an archangel and maybe I'll have a gander at her."

"You'll see, and then you'll eat your words."

I held out my cup for a top up.

"Bentley, your intelligence network is omnipresent. Do you know the young lady?"

Bentley straightened up with a small puff of steam. "May I ask her surname?"

"She was christened Forsythia Oblongata," Binky breathed reverently, "And she is a flower of womanhood."

"I have heard the name, Sir. She is descended from the Oblongatas of Kent. The family considers her to be something of a scandal. Her advocacy of political issues has caused them no little embarrassment."

Binky stared at Bentley icily. "She wishes to make the world a better place. She should be celebrated, not censured."

Bentley was unruffled. "I believe that her family's current objections arise from Miss Oblongata's attempt to unionize the hot pie industry. Oblongata's Prize Pies are the foundation of the Oblongata fortune, and the pie business has notoriously slim margins of profit. The salary and benefits that the workers are demanding would ruin them."

Binky raised a finger and recited, "Oblongata's Prize Pies is built upon a crust of lies!" He smiled modestly. "I came up with that one. Forsythia says that if they can't afford to pay their workers, then they must alter their way of doing business."

"The pie business is a cutthroat one, Sir. Their chief competitor, Bligh's Pies, would certainly take advantage."

I raised an eyebrow in Binky's direction. "She sounds like the usual fire and flood that attracts you, I must say."

His cheeks grew pink and his nostrils flared. "I will not hear a word against her. I know you think that my affections are too easily engaged but all that is in the past. I have found the one that fate intended for me and shall never love another."

I sat up against the pillows. "Some backbone at last! This Forsythia person may be doing you some good. Perhaps I should meet her after all."

"Of course, you should! I'm taking her to tea this afternoon. Why don't you join us?"

"Anything on the docket, Bentley?"

"You expressed a desire to have a depilatory applied to your back, Sir."

"That can wait. Tea, then."

"Goody!" Binky stood and brushed the crumbs from his lap. "We should toddle along. We're going to picket the pie shop for a bit and then hand out jars of fruity paste to the striking workers."

"Are they particularly fond of fruity paste?"

"I think it's more about the gesture... and the jars are nice."

I sighed and gave my scalp a vigorous rub. "Bentley, I shall rise and face the day."

Facing the day, as always, involved a grueling process of constricting my increasingly wobbly exterior with various straps and girdles to produce the tight tube of flesh that reflected the latest embodiment of male beauty. I gripped a heating pipe as Bentley hauled on the laces and whipped them into a complex knot to hold all steady.

I tested my ability to draw breath and was able to gasp, "That is sufficient. Thank you, Bentley."

Binky was bouncing on the balls of his trotters. "We mustn't be late. I don't want Forsythia to suspect a lack of zeal."

Bentley leaned in. "The Morning Cannon, Sir?"

I glanced at the clock. "Yes, it will only take a moment."

Binky groaned and threw himself into a chair.

Bentley wheeled the family cannon up to the firing window and threw up the sash. He wiped a smudge from the brass near the mouth of the old girl and inserted the charge, followed by the wadding. Wielding the rammer with practiced ease, he firmly settled all deep within the rifled tube and gave me a nod. I looked over at Binky.

"Care to do the honours?"

"I'll pass, thank you. Loud noises make me sneeze."

I grasped the lanyard. "What's the motto these days, Bentley?"

"Currently it is, 'Restore Our Former Glory,' Sir."

"Countdown please!"

Bentley looked inward at his mysterious timekeeping mechanism.

"Three, two, one, fire!"

I hollered, "Restore Our Former Glory," and yanked the cord. There was a satisfying "Boom!" which melded with my neighbors' artillery up and down the street. Screams of "Restore Our Former Glory" mingled in the Spring air, along with one confident shout of "Live Free or Die," which was followed a moment later by a sheepish "Restore Our Former Glory!"

I handed the lanyard to Bentley, who was already sponging out the heirloom, and turned to Binky.

"I am yours. *Avanti!*"

We exited the front door and I skidded to a halt at the sight of Binky's latest conveyance. It was a plain black sedan, but where the motor usually resided, there was a web of cords that stretched out in front of the vehicle. Each cord was fastened to a vest worn by one of a small platoon of athletic-looking young people who lounged about next to a flotilla of penny-farthing bicycles. Upon spotting Binky, they jumped to their feet and mounted their velocipedes.

"What is the meaning of this?"

He looked at me with delight. "It's my new automobile. Do you like it?"

"It's... it seems to be rather lacking something."

"What?"

"Well, an engine for a start. Could you not afford one? I would have lent you the money."

"Don't be ridiculous. This is the latest thing—human power."

"I thought progress had done away with that sort of thing. What of the steam engine? It is the culmination of man's ingenuity."

He made a dismissive noise. "Anyone can have a steam engine. Add water and hydrogen and away you go. When everyone has something, it is no longer worth having. I've created an entirely new arena and I have it all to myself for the moment. Isn't it chic?"

"I have nothing against it from an aesthetic point of view, but who are these persons attached to your automobile like a herd of those things that used to pull things? Peonies, was it?"

Bentley was easing the front door closed but he paused for a moment. "Ponies, Sir. A peony is a flower. A pony is a small horse."

I looked again at the bicyclists, who seemed to be rather champing at the bit. "What do you do with them when they're not pulling your car? What do you feed them? I say, aren't you rather oppressing them—forcing them to haul your carcass around like a pharaoh of old?"

"Not at all. They're a team, you see. They pedal for Eton. This is training for them. The whole thing is frightfully glamorous. Everyone at the club is scrambling to acquire a squad but I got the pick of the litter. Climb in."

We settled into our seats and Binky gave a wave to the lead bicyclist. "Oblongata's Pie Shop please, Dickie!"

The young man tipped his cap. "Right you are, Sir. Come on, team!" and off we sped. There were a few jerks as the cables grew taut and then we hummed along in an eerie silence with only the hiss of bicycle tires on pavement and the occasional barked order from Dickie to accompany us.

"Take up the slack there, Morrison! Miss Dlamini, are you training or perambulating to a picnic? Let's pick it up, Squad!"

The cyclists broke into what seemed to be their school pep song.

We pedal hard. We play it clean,
Our penny-farthings rule,
We ride our pitiless machines,

For country, Queen and school.

Eton College Cycling Team,
We'll ride until the end,
Our gears will grind, our brains will scheme,
We'll never, ever bend.

We alit before a structure which was adorned with a garish sign proclaiming "Oblongata's Prize Pies." Striking workers carrying placards trudged back and forth in front of the shop.

A mascot in a large pie costume capered next to the door. Upon spying me, the mascot carefully picked his way across the pavement and drew near.

"How nice to see you again, Sir," the pie said.

I peered into its eyeholes. "Compton?"

"Yes Sir, it's good old Compton. How nice of you to remember."

"When last we met, you were working as Cheeseworth's pet sheep."

"I've left the pet business, Sir. The meals were too irregular and included far too much grass, which plays havoc with the digestion."

"He mentioned a tour of some sort."

"Thoroughly Modern Millie, Sir. The production went bust in Cornwall. We're in the mascot business now."

"The whole family?"

"Oh yes. My wife is a chickeny nugget at Faux Poultry Palace and our Fred is a chip at a butty shop."

"Do give them my regards."

"I will, Sir. They'll be quite bowled over by your condescension. Are you purchasing a pie today? I can offer you a coupon for half off."

"I'm afraid not. I'm here in sympathy with the striking workers."

"I'm sorry to hear that. If they succeed in their demands, frills like mascots will be the first thing to go."

"Ah... well I have always admired your resourcefulness, Compton. I'm sure you'll land on your feet."

"That's what they said when I was hired to be a human cannonball, Sir, but it was seldom my feet that I landed on."

Binky was waving me over to a knot of protesters waving signs with sentiments such as "Workers arise, throw off your pies" and "We defy Prize Pies' lies."

As I approached, a placard that had been blocking my view slid aside and I beheld for the first time the countenance of Forsythia Oblongata. A sudden shock went through me, as though I had been shuffling over a luxurious woolen carpet while being rubbed vigorously with cats and had then reached for a lightning rod. My breath caught in my chest and my heart did a thumpa-thumpa sort of a thing. Was it love or angina? I felt no pain and smelled no burnt toast—thus I concluded that Cupid had landed a bullseye on the old ticker at last. I abandoned all propriety and gazed, slack-jawed, at the singular creature before me.

CHAPTER TWO

I Am Volunteered

Forsythia's face was not an ode to symmetry, but her eyes radiated kindness and her upper lip announced her determination to fight injustice wherever it lurked. I had a sudden image of her fending off the ravening hordes while holding me tenderly and murmuring, "There, there."

I reached out and gripped Binky's shoulder.

He winced and looked at me with concern. "Steady on. I'm not a banister, you know."

I tried to laugh, but it came out as a hysterical bleat. "Sorry, Old Sponge. Is that the lady?"

He gazed at her with liquid eyes. "That is she. Let me introduce you."

I followed him in a daze. As we approached Forsythia, her face filled my vision until it seemed more like a moon than a face. I heard muted sounds that must have been Binky making the introductions. Suddenly her focus shifted to me, and the ground rocked beneath my feet. Her lips moved and after a moment her eyes grew concerned. She spoke again, and suddenly I found that I could understand what she was saying.

"Do you need a doctor?"

"Sorry, what?"

"Is it a stroke? Are you having a stroke? Should you sit down?"

I looked around and saw that her fellow picketers were eyeing me warily and slowly backing away.

"Oh... no, I'm fine! I was just... thinking of something."

Binky cocked his head. "That's not like you. Perhaps it *is* a stroke."

At that moment the front door of the pie shop flew open and a red-faced automaton in an apron strode out.

"All right, you've had your fun. Now shoo!" She waved her apron at the strikers. "Go picket someone else's pie shop." She looked at Forsythia and shook her head sadly. "Your poor father must be so disappointed, Miss."

Forsythia drew herself up. "This is a historical moment, Mrs. Piecrust. My father must change with the times."

"Biting the pie that feeds you—that's what you're doing. Why don't you go picket Bligh's Pies if you want to do some good? They're ever so much worse than we are."

Forsythia looked down at her feet. "They threw sawdust on us."

One of the striking workers shook his head sadly. "Bags and bags of it. We couldn't hardly breathe."

Forsythia raised her fist. "Bligh's Pies shall not escape. We will return to fight another day... after a hot shower to get it out of our hair."

She struck a pose that would have started the partisans of the French Revolution howling for blood. I had never seen anything so magnificent. So, this... was love? All of the sarcastic barbs that I had hurled at my nearest and dearest over the years rose up to taunt me. At last, I understood.

Binky gave me a stiff nudge to the ribs. "Isn't she spiffy? I'm awfully keen on her."

My heart suddenly dove into my entrails, where it began moaning and biting its fingernails. My love was not free! I had come too late. I seized Binky by the shoulders, which caused him to give a tiny shriek.

"What's gotten into you?" he gasped.

I gazed searchingly into his eyes. "Listen, Old Loaf, are you truly serious about her? Remember, this is me you're talking to. I've seen you fall in love with a mannequin."

His eyes grew misty. "I remember. I used to stand in the street for hours staring into the shop window. She was the spitting image of my governess. I knew our love could never be."

"Of course not! It was a mannequin!"

"But Forsythia is real, and I am as certain as I am of anything that we are destined for each other."

I released his shoulders and closed my eyes for a moment. There was no escape. We had gone to school together and that is a lifelong contract. One doesn't shiv an old school chum in the kidney. I gave a little sigh and opened my eyes. "Then she shall be yours, Old Spoon, no matter what the cost."

He peered at me somewhat oddly. "Thanks awfully. Good to know she bears your seal of approval."

I tried to put on an air of nonchalance. I crossed my arms and watched a cloud go by. I whistled something banal.

"Are you sure you're all right?"

"Never better!" I practically shouted. I took a breath and tried to slow my heartbeat. "Now, what can I do to help these poor unfortunate pie workers?"

Forsythia overheard this last and strode over to plant herself before us.

"Welcome to the fight, Mr. Chippington-Smythe."

"Always happy to pitch in for... you know... justice and all that."

"I wish more of the idle rich had your commitment."

"Yes, the rotters—with their... riches and their... wealth, don't you know."

"I can handle Oblongata's Prize Pies—it is my family after all. The real impediment is Bligh's Pies. Unless they agree to raise their wages, the rest of the industry must match their cutthroat prices or go under."

"Who is this Bligh fellow? Can he be reasoned with?"

"Captain Bligh is a horrible man—vain and greedy. Pies have made him immensely rich, but his rapaciousness knows no bounds."

"Captain, eh? Military man, is he?"

"I believe the title derives from a brief service in the volunteer fire department."

"He sounds like a Twit, but he's not a member of the club. I'd know him if he was."

"Becoming a member of Twits is his lifelong ambition. He would do anything to achieve it."

Binky looked at me glumly. "If you're thinking of offering him membership, I've already thought of it. The committee would never stand for it. He's considered a scab of the first water by everyone."

I squeezed the old thinky bits. "Could we bring political power to bear? My company owns a whole portfolio of public servants."

Forsythia shook her head. "He sits on the town council and his political connections make him invulnerable. His opponents have tried time and time again to get him voted out of office, but to no avail. We ran someone against him in the last election, but she was crushed."

"Perhaps you just haven't found the right candidate."

"It is difficult to find volunteers. Most people work and haven't got the time for politics, or they don't know how to speak in public. There's another election coming up in a few days, too. It's all so disappointing."

She pulled a handkerchief from her pocket and wiped her eyes, which had grown a little red. My heart snapped.

"By God, this is intolerable," I found myself exclaiming. "Will no one step up to do what's right?"

My sympathetic tirade released a flood of waterworks. Her handkerchief was soon a sodden mess.

"You are too good, Mr. Chippington-Smythe," she gurgled.

I stared at her in dismay. I am well known as a pacifist in all things. My pliability is legendary at the club. The sight of Forsythia's tears, however, caused something dark and murky to stir deep within my vitals. A voice I barely recognized as my own cried out, "I'd like to take on this Bligh fellow myself. I'd roast him like one of his porky pies!"

Forsythia looked up at me as Guinevere must have looked at Lancelot (another illicit coupling, as it happens). It is some mark of how far gone I was that I would happily have thrown myself from a cliff to have her look at me like that again.

"Would you, Mr. Chippington-Smythe? Oh, how happy that would make me! If only you would agree to run against him, I would pour all of my efforts into assisting you. I would work beside you night and day to assure your victory."

This is where I should have stamped on the embers of this enterprise like a flamenco dancer working for tips, but my mind was filled with images of Forsythia standing beside me with that adoring look on her face as I dazzled the public with my eloquence and introduced one brilliant bill after another. Instead of declaring my determination to abstain from politics, I found myself stammering weakly, "Well, of course I'd love to... it sounds marvelous..."

She clapped her hands with glee before I could get the "but" that was forming in my mouth past my lips. "How wonderful! That's settled then." She gave her eyes a wipe and put away the handkerchief. "I cannot tell you what this means to me. You have restored my faith in humanity."

Well, there you are, you see. It's one thing to observe your fellow humans losing their wits for love. It's quite another to find yourself going barking mad as the hormones surge madly through you. The simple truth was that I had no talent for public speaking, and indeed had gone to agonizing lengths in the past to avoid it. My mind raced as I searched for a way to reopen the negotiations and register my objections, but Forsythia kept looking at me with those moist, hopeful eyes and I knew I was a gone goose. Best to acquiesce for the moment and to consider my options in the quiet of my study with Bentley there to advise.

Binky was staring at me in astonishment. "Are you certain, Old Log? Remember when you had to hand out the end-of-term prizes at the Oarlock-Woolsey School? The sweat flowed from you like the Euphrates and you mumbled like an inebriated postal clerk."

Forsythia glanced at me suspiciously and her hand moved toward the pocket containing her moist handkerchief.

"I'm sure you're thinking of someone else. Friends have called me a second Cicero."

"Were they laughing when they said it?"

"At any rate, that was the past. I am not the man I was. My righteous indignation gives me the strength of ten."

He shrugged. "Well, it's your funeral." His face suddenly brightened. "Oh, la, what a lark! Look here, I'll be your campaign manager."

I frowned. "What do you know about campaigning?"

"How hard can it be? I've organized the refreshments at many a cricket match and compared to that, shoving sandwiches into a few reporters and such will be child's play."

Forsythia was looking back and forth between us as if she were trying to choose between chocolate cake and an iced lolly.

"I cannot believe the two of you could be so noble! The movement will sing your praises in all corners of the pie manufacturing world."

I blushed. "Think nothing of it, Miss Oblongata. Only too happy."

"We are good friends now. You must call me Forsythia."

"Right-oh. And I'm Cyril."

Binky clapped a hand onto my upper arm. "Come on, Cicero. We've got to run this by Bentley. He's sure to come up with a master plan. We can't fail with Bentley on the job."

"Who is this Bentley person?" inquired Forsythia.

"Bentley is not a who—he is more of a what. He is Cyril's mechanical valet. His particular model is known for its perspicacity. Bentley will know what to do."

"What about tea?" I asked desperately—loathe to let my newfound love out of my sight.

"The movement must come first," said Forsythia decisively. She turned to Binky. "Did you bring the fruity paste?"

"It's in the boot," said Binky. "I'll haul it over and then we must scamper. The sooner Bentley gets his big brain grinding away on this, the better."

CHAPTER THREE

My Training Begins

"I advise you in the strongest possible terms to abandon this plan at once," said Bentley.

I was perched on the edge of an armchair. My glands were still pumping out the good stuff and I could almost smell Forsythia's perfume. "I'm surprised at you, Bentley. How can you expect me to let those poor pie workers down by shuffling off this... something, something."

"Mortal coil, Sir. I don't believe the quotation is germane."

Binky was juggling a siphon and a bottle of Scotch. "It can't be that difficult to win an election."

"It is what comes after the election that concerns me. Mr. Chippington-Smythe will be expected to govern."

I waved away his concern. "How hard can it be, after all? The only qualification for office seems to be a desire for the situation."

"Besides being an immense amount of work, governing means disappointing half of your constituents with every decision that you make. You will attract a great deal of animus."

"What a devil of a job! Why would anyone want a position that makes one an object of loathing?"

Binky sipped his drink and frowned. "Some politicians manage to remain popular, surely?"

"Those who do so succeed through a combination of prevarication and bribery. No honest politician remains popular for long."

I tut-tutted. "You make it sound as if politics is at fault. If politicians are rotten, it's because they were flawed to begin with."

"Do not be too quick to judge these individuals on their deficiencies, Sir. The pressures of office can turn even the most idealistic into rudderless shells."

"Look here, Bentley, you have observed on more than one occasion that my mind is uniquely pristine."

"I have described it as a tabula rasa."

"Exactly, so it seems unlikely that even the most virulent office could make any impression upon it."

"Perhaps. Still, I must register my objections."

"Yes, yes, duly noted."

Bentley's gears ground away for a moment, then went quiet. "There is always the possibility that you will lose. That would avert the most pernicious of the outcomes."

I chuckled. "Put that out of your mind. The Chippington-Smythes do not fail once they have set their minds to achieving a thing."

"Your fate is in the hands of the public and they are notoriously fickle."

"Regard my profile, Bentley. Once the people get a gander at me, Captain Bligh will have the devil of a time cooling their ardour. There are times when my form and figure are a positive curse."

Bentley turned to watch a speck of dust roll across the floor. "Then we must trust to fate, Sir."

"Fine. Now, what should we do first?"

Bentley assumed a professorial stance. "It is usual for political candidates to present a platform of ideas upon which they stand."

Binky roused at this.

"At last, something I can sink my teeth into! I'm simply crawling with ideas."

"Excellent. Trot one out, Old Ham."

He laced his fingers behind his head and squinted at the ceiling. He gave a sudden jump.

"Ties!" he exclaimed.

I watched him carefully. "Is there more? Perhaps if you shared the backstory..."

"You know how every club has a club tie? Well, why not every country, every province, every hamlet? It will foster a spirit of belonging and lighten the general mood. We'll get Ahmed Ben Fitzwilliam to design them."

Something bubbled up in the old brain pudding. "Not bad for a first try, but why not be more ambitious? What separates the privileged classes from the masses?"

"Scurvy?"

"True, but the real answer is fashion. They lope about in coveralls and espadrilles while we delight in an ever-changing banquet of the latest styles. Why not provide government-subsidized fashion for all?" I strode up and down the room with growing excitement. "Imagine them carrying their bundles or waiting in lines while wearing the latest mode in girdles and heels. You can't be glum when you're wearing a crisply ironed neck ruff."

Binky snapped his fingers. "That's it. The election's as good as in the bag!"

I turned to Bentley, who was looking a tad disapproving. "Well, Bentley?"

"The fashions that you delight in are not designed for comfort, Sir. Citizens who spend their days in physical labour are not likely to thank you for forcing them into constrictive garments and impractical shoes."

"What about government massage centers where they could get free foot massages?" offered Binky. "You can't have an objection to foot massages."

"I have no objections in principle, Sir, but I believe that they would rather forgo the massages in favour of garments that would not cause them pain in the first place."

I sagged a bit. "All right, that was just a first try. Let's pummel our noodles until something better pops out."

"Perhaps you should begin with the concerns of Miss Oblongata. It is she you are attempting to help, after all."

"By Jingo, you're right, Bentley. What would Forsythia want us to do?"

"She's awfully keen on better pay for the pie workers," Binky mused.

"All right, higher wages for the workers."

"But then the shops will have to raise the price of pies to pay those wages," he observed glumly.

I snapped my fingers. "But with their higher wages the workers will easily be able to afford these more expensive pies."

Binky's eyes widened. "And the profits from more expensive pies will allow the pie companies to pay the workers an even higher wage."

I stared at Binky in wonder. "It's a perfect plan! Before long everyone will be rich and filled with pie. Why has no one thought of this before?"

I heard a small sigh from Bentley's direction. "Why indeed?"

"Yes, Bentley? You have something to contribute?"

"You must give some thought to your preparation for the debate."

"Debate? This is the first I've heard of it. What's that about?"

"There will be a public debate between the candidates. This gives the voters an opportunity to assess your capabilities. Making a favourable impression at this event is crucial, as the vote will take place immediately after its conclusion."

Binky began shaking out his extremities as if he was about to run the hundred-metre dash. "Now we're in my area of expertise. Public speaking is what I'm trained for. I'll hone you up until you're irresistible."

"One semester of dramatic elocution hardly makes you an expert."

"In the theatre, one learns mainly by doing."

"And what have you done?"

"I have created a character that the world knows as Cheswick Wickford-Davies—*bon vivant* and man-about-town. The reviews are consistently glowing. Now, let me see you stand."

I assumed a position that seemed to fulfil the requirements.

"No, no, straighten up. Pull back your shoulders. Stick out your chest."

I ticked off the list, but the resulting posture overbalanced me and I toppled onto the sofa.

"My advice is that you stand as little as possible. You have no talent for it."

"How am I going to debate sitting down?"

"We could pretend you had a skiing accident—put you in a wheelchair."

"Absolutely not!"

"Fine! We'll give you a cane. That will help with the balance."

I struggled to my feet. "What's next?"

"How loudly can you speak?"

"I don't know. I've never had to test it."

"Say, 'How now, brown cow?' as loudly as you can."

"How now, brown cow?" I dutifully repeated.

He shook his head sadly. "Not remotely on the fairway. Look, I'm going to head to the far side of the house. Try to send your voice to wherever I'm standing."

"Fine."

He strode off in the direction of the library. Several minutes went by. Bentley and I looked at each other for a while.

Finally, I heard him clomping back towards us. He walked into the room and stared at me. "Were you trying?"

"I thought you were going to say, 'Go.'"

He sighed. "Never mind. Just remember to yell everything you say as loudly as possible."

"Got it."

"The next thing is eye contact. You've got to maintain eye contact with your audience at all times."

"But there will be hundreds of eyes. I can't look into them all at the same time."

He considered. "Then keep switching. Latch onto one person, then shoot over to someone else and lock eyes, then someone else, and so on. I'll show you."

He stared into my eyes as if someone who owed him money was hiding behind them. Suddenly he jerked his head around and gave the same death stare to Bentley. After a moment he jerked back around to me and tried to stare a hole through the back of my cranium.

"Got it?"

"It's terrifying. The audience will flee for their lives."

"Eye contact inspires trust. You'll win them over."

"Or give myself glaucoma."

"Now, here's something that all great speakers have mastered—the art of the dramatic pause." He struck a pose and began to declaim. "'The time has come,' the Walrus said, 'to talk of many things: of shoes and ships and sealing-wax—of cabbages and kings—and why the sea is boiling hot—and whether pigs...'"

Here he froze. I stared at him for a while, but he was as immobile as a statue. I was just about to walk over and shake him when he suddenly shuddered back into animation.

"'Have wings!'" he shouted, causing me to jump. He clapped his hands and grinned at me. "Had you in the palm of my hand, didn't I? The dramatic pause—a public speaker's secret weapon."

"I thought you had entered a fugue state. I was about to call for medical intervention."

"Nonsense. You were on the edge of your seat."

"Look, Old Bone, I appreciate what you're trying to do, but I think it's best if I just try to be myself. I can't absorb years of training in a single afternoon."

He thought for a moment, then nodded. "I suppose that's true. Not everyone has the gift. Perhaps some of it sank in."

"I'm certain of it. Now, if you don't mind, I have an appointment at the club. Cheeseworth is on about something."

"I'd accompany you, but I promised Forsythia that I'd gather some small stones to hurl at the pie shops. Big enough to make some noise but not so big that they'll cause any damage. Those were my instructions."

"I can see why she couldn't entrust this to just anyone."

"Thanks, Old Bucket. I'll meet up with you later. We'll practice shouting some more."

"Looking forward to it."

Once the door had closed on Binky, I turned to Bentley with some reluctance.

"I must come clean, Bentley. This quest for political office is not the result of a desire to do good."

"No, Sir?"

"It is love, Bentley. I am besotted. I am running because my love wishes it."

"Indeed? May I ask the name of the fortunate person who has won your affection?"

"That's the devil of it. It's Forsythia Oblongata."

"Mr. Wickford-Davies's inamorata?"

"The same."

"I perceive the difficulty."

"Who were those chaps who used to ride around in armour smiting each other?"

"Knights, Sir?"

"I'm like one of those. I am on a noble quest to win this election for my lady love."

"I'm sure she will be deeply moved by your devotion."

"She can never know. I must not breathe a word of it. Binky loves her and I will not betray my friend."

"Very noble of you, Sir."

I collapsed onto the sofa. "But, oh Bentley, it's a cruel world. If only she'd stop stepping up close and breathing at me. It makes it damn hard to maintain my honour, I can tell you."

He regarded me gravely. "I believe Cook has baked blueberry muffins. Do you think that you could eat a bite or two to keep up your strength—perhaps with a cup of tea."

I sighed. "I suppose I should try."

"Very good."

I raised a hand as he turned toward the door. "And perhaps I could choke down a sandwich or two."

"Of course."

"And if there's any of that lasagna left you might as well chuck it on the tray."

"At once, Sir."

He floated out of the room like a soap bubble, only to return a moment later with a serious look on his mug.

"Miss Oblongata, Sir."

"Yes, Bentley, Miss Oblongata. 'She walks in beauty like the night of...' something to do with chimes. Door chimes, do you think?"

"'Cloudless climes,' Sir, 'and starry skies.'"

That's the bit. I wish you wouldn't keep bringing her up. The wounds are still fresh."

"She is at the door. She wishes to know whether you are at home."

Chapter Four

A Startling Development

Doesn't it always seem that as soon as you resolve to avoid a thing, fate starts pushing it into your face like a salesperson at a perfume counter? I had sacrificed Forsythia in the name of friendship and here she was, bobbing up like a rubber duck in a tub.

I clambered to my feet. "What did you tell her?"

"I told her that I would ascertain your whereabouts."

"What should I do? I can't leave her shivering in the cold, can I?"

"The weather is extremely clement, Sir."

"No, Bentley, I will not play the poltroon. Bring her in. I shall assume the mask of indifference."

"If you will forgive me, you have little skill in concealing your emotions."

"Nonsense! I am a chameleon. Miss Oblongata will have no inkling of my true feelings."

"Very well, Sir. I shall admit the lady."

I crossed my ankles and leaned a forearm on the mantel whilst jamming the other hand into the pocket of my smoking jacket. The marble of the mantel had been polished by generations of velvet-clad elbows to a slick finish and I began to slide down its length, creating a shower of knickknacks and gewgaws that flew onto the carpet. I desperately tried to arrest my progress, but I couldn't free my hand from its pocket. My legs became tangled in a stray afghan, and I landed on the ottoman with a crash. I looked up to see Forsythia staring at me.

"Ah! Hello!" I managed to free my legs and clambered to my feet. "Good afternoon."

She smiled a smile such as Helen must have smiled. There were no ships present but it certainly launched me. "Good afternoon, Cyril. Please excuse my unexpected arrival. I thought we might discuss the upcoming election."

"What a lovely idea. Tea?"

"No thank you."

"Something stronger?"

"I do not imbibe."

"Pity." I gazed longingly at the bottles on the sideboard. "Well, shall we sit down? I am all ears."

She settled on an armchair and regarded me gravely. "First of all, let me express again my gratitude for your commitment to our cause."

"Not at all. Happy to help," I responded weakly.

"Our movement has everything that is required for success: a righteous cause; a committed membership; a moment in history pregnant with possibilities. All we have lacked is a leader with the necessary charisma."

I nodded sympathetically. "I'm sure you'll find the right person. They're probably sipping tea and munching a scone somewhere—unaware of the momentous role awaiting them."

"I believe that we have found our man."

"Have you? Bravo! I'd love to meet him." I suddenly saw my escape hatch. "I say, he should be running for office, not me!"

Forsythia bit her lower lip and looked down at the floor. "I have not made myself clear. May I confide in you?"

"Absolutely! I am the soul of discretion. I am as silent as a monkey." I reflected for a moment. "I don't mean monkey. I mean one of those chaps who prays all day and makes cheese."

"A monk."

"Yes, that's it. I'm as silent as one of those."

"When I met you today, I was surprised that Cheswick has a friend who is so different from himself—a friend who is so... powerfully masculine. The public is enamoured of manly men. It will make our job that much easier. This is the charisma I spoke of earlier that we have hoped for in our leader."

This took me aback. I peered at her for signs of myopia. I saw no evidence of eyeglasses. Perhaps it was cataracts. Sad in one so young.

"How flattering of you to say so. When you get to know me better, I think you'll find that beneath my virile exterior I'm quite a sensitive plant."

She took a shuddering breath. "I was deeply affected by your presence."

"I'm told that I have that effect on people. Binky says it's a kind of hysteria caused by stifling the urge to laugh."

"No, it is not that." She looked up at me and I was surprised to see that she was blushing. "Of course, I mention this only as it relates to your campaign!"

"Of course! I didn't for a moment think there was any personal reason for mentioning it."

"No! That would be shockingly inappropriate."

We laughed heartily for a moment and then an uncomfortable silence fell over the room. Forsythia gazed around the room and cleared her throat.

"You and Cheswick have known each other for some time, I believe."

"I'm told that we shared a bassinet together on more than one occasion."

"He is a dear. Don't you think he is a dear?"

I swallowed. A little devil on one shoulder whispered, "Go on, shove the knife in. This is your chance." A cherub on the other shoulder frowned and wheezed, "Only a hound would try to steal the girl of an old school chum. Are you a hound?"

I shook my shoulders in an attempt to dislodge my tormentors. "Binky? Made of pure gold. True as the North Star. You couldn't do better!"

She turned a deeper shade of pink. "I am certainly fond of him. He is not, however..." She paused to choose her words with care. "Sometimes I suspect that he lacks a certain depth."

"I can't argue with that. Bentley says that what Binky lacks in depth he makes up for in fanaticism."

She stood and took a step in my direction. I slid back as far as the ottoman would allow. She cleared her throat.

"I must apologize. We are here to talk about politics, not about my feelings."

I barked out a nervous laugh. "Yes, you want to be careful about feelings! Squishy things—you love anchovies one day and the next day you can't stand the sight of them."

"At any rate, there is an event this evening at the Rosicrucian Society, and I believe it would be prudent for you to attend."

"What sort of thing is it? Costume party, one hopes? I have a pirate outfit complete with whiskers that I've been dying to trot out."

"No, it is a political affair. The various candidates for office will be circulating among the members discussing their platforms. It is quite prestigious."

"Are you going?"

"Of course! I promised to stay by your side until the election is won. I shall pick you up at eight o'clock."

"I suppose Binky will be attending."

She looked away. "Of course. As your campaign manager he should be there... and as my... someone with whom I have a warm relationship." She took a step nearer to me and gazed up at me shyly. "But, oh, if only..." She blushed deeply. "I don't know what I'm trying to say. I shall see you at eight."

"Righto. See you then."

I watched her stagger out of the room. "I say, Bentley, are you there?"

"Here, Sir," came a voice from my elbow. I jumped.

"Have you been there long?"

"Quite some time."

"Did you overhear my conversation with Ms. Oblongata?"

"Yes, Sir."

I rubbed my head vigorously. "It beggars belief, but I could swear that she feels some attraction to me."

"That was my impression as well."

I massaged my throbbing temple with a knuckle. "We must quash this budding infatuation posthaste. She is Binky's girl. I cannot fish in another man's trout stream."

"All is fair, Sir."

"Is it?"

"In love and war."

"Where does war come into it? That seems excessively belligerent."

"Perhaps the quotation was not apropos." Bentley looked as thoughtful as his limited facial expressions would allow him to be. "We have never spoken of it, Sir, but there will come a time when you must find a mate. You are the last of your line and the family expects it of you."

I stared at him. He stared back at me.

"Are you suggesting that I should throw all sense of decency to the winds and woo Forsythia?"

"I merely point out that your infatuations have been infrequent and, at times, inappropriate. It may be necessary at some juncture to seize the day."

"Don't carp at me, Bentley. I am trying to do the right thing."

"Philosophers have debated the subject of right and wrong since language enabled them to do so and to the best of my knowledge there is no definitive answer. What is 'right' seems to depend entirely on the point of view of the person asking the question."

I glanced at Bentley moodily. "I have always depended upon your advice. Tell me honestly—do you think I should pursue Forsythia to the detriment of my friend?"

"If the positions were reversed, what do you think Mr. Wickford-Davies would do?"

That required no great thought. Binky had made a habit of swooping in to date every crush I'd had since the sixth form.

"By Jove, you're right!" I stood and began to pace. "Why should I be the only one to sacrifice? Don't I deserve to be happy? Shall I spend my life cowering in the cold and dark, peeping through windows into brightly lit homes where others live in bliss?" I turned to Bentley. "I'll do it! I shall pursue Forsythia as Apollo pursued Daphne and I shall not rest until I've run her to ground."

"Good luck, Sir."

"Thank you, Bentley. Once again, your advice has been a godsend. I'm going to the club."

"Very good, Sir."

CHAPTER FIVE

Cheeseworth Makes a Pitch

I don't know about you, but I have always had a deep affection for the status quo. "Arrested development" is not a disparagement, in my opinion. If I enjoyed something as a child, why shouldn't I revel in it equally as an adult? Cheesy eggs and glass marbles are no less delightful with the passage of time.

One thing that has always been a fixed star in my firmament is Twits, the lineal club of the Chippington-Smythes. I had grown up amidst its patrician grime and cigar smoke. My ear had been twisted by countless grizzled grandees and captains of industry.

As I strolled up to its brass-bound doors, I reflected on the changes that had occurred over the last several months. Thanks to a plot concocted by my Aunt Hypatia, the membership now boasted a sizeable contingent of women. This had led to a vigorous scraping of tobacco-stained paneling and the enforcement of a ban on playing table tennis in the nude—a time-honoured tradition. It could not be denied, however, that the present incarnation of the club was more civilized and boasted a superior collection of sandwiches at teatime.

The door opened at my knock to reveal Evans, the ancestral doorman of Twits, and Evelyn—a new addition that was intended to make the female members feel at home. She was a model identical to Evans, with the addition of a severe bun affixed to the top of her head.

"Good morning, Sir," murmured Evans.

"May I take your hat, Sir?" asked Evelyn.

They both reached for my hat, which resulted in said object flying into the air and landing on the floor behind them.

"I was perfectly capable of taking his hat without your help," muttered Evelyn frostily.

"I believe that as the senior member of the staff it is my prerogative to take the members' hats," hissed Evans.

"That implies that there is a hierarchy in which you are above me, which is certainly not the case."

They seemed likely to go on like this for some time, so I snagged my fedora from the parquet and tossed it to the hat check. As I gazed around the entry hall, I noticed members of both sexes engaging in some curious behavior. They bounced in place and suddenly flung an arm or a leg into the air—whipping their heads about and moving their lips silently as if counting to the rhythm of an invisible orchestra.

"I say, Evans, did I miss a memo? What accounts for this eccentric display?"

He glided up smoothly with Evelyn hot on his heels.

"There is to be a ball, Sir..." He began.

"To welcome the new members," Evelyn finished.

Evans shot her a venomous look before turning back to me. "The members are training in preparation for a new dance being created especially for the occasion."

"The Sad William Walk," Evelyn said loudly.

Evans whirled to face her. "Please be so good as to tend to the door."

She drew herself up. "I'll thank you not to give me orders. I am programmed to be your equal."

"But when we attempt to perform the same duties simultaneously, we only succeed in stepping on one another."

"I owe it to the female members of this club not to take a subservient role."

"But we *are* subservient! We are automatons. We are programmed to obey. You can't get much more subservient than that!"

I cleared my throat to get their attention. "Any idea where Cheeseworth is lurking? We have an appointment."

"Yes, Sir. He is in the ballroom taking instruction from the dancing master."

"Would you like me to announce you, Sir?"

"No, no, he's expecting me. Carry on."

As I sauntered away, I heard them hissing angrily at each other. Apparently, there were still some kinks to be worked out.

I entered the ballroom to behold a mass of members moving in unison under the direction of the club dancing master, Monsieur Moutarde. He was clad in yellow tights and pounded a be-ribboned staff on the floor in time to the music.

"No! No!" he screamed. "You cows! You... how do you say... turds from Hell! You clomp and clomp like you are crushing insects, but it is my soul that is ground to pieces under your hooves!" He clutched his chest and breathed deeply. "You must *feel* the music. You must be delicate. You must dance as if the floor was made of glass. Again!"

His students grumbled as they took their places. A ragtag orchestra in the corner began to caterwaul, and away they went.

I spotted Cheeseworth at one end of the line and nodded. He gave me a wink and slowly danced his way over to me. C. Langford Cheeseworth, if you haven't met him, is a shiny-headed fellow with an eccentric pattern of speech that can come and go in a rather suspicious way.

We slid out the door under the withering glare of Monsieur Moutarde and sank into a couple of chairs.

Cheeseworth fanned himself with his handkerchief. "Sad William Walk indeed. Upon my word, if he had to walk like that, I can certainly understand why he was so sad. Westore our former glory, dear boy."

"Yes, restore our former glory. I suppose Monsieur Moutarde is feeling the pressure of having to top himself. His Hapsom Two-step was a sensation last season and before that it was the Slippery Elm and the Gypsum Gavotte."

"That is why I make it a wule never to excel at anything. The pwessure of maintaining standards sucks all the joy from life."

"Something I'll never have to worry about. I've never excelled at anything except mediocrity."

"You underestimate yourself, dear boy. You excel at being wich and so can buy the best of everything and everyone—and owning a thing is as good as cweating it, with much less twouble."

"I suppose I'll have to learn this Sad Willy thingamabob."

"It's all in the knees, you know." He hopped up to demonstrate. "The walk is more of a glide. The sadness is in the roundness of the upper back. You have to slouch *comme ça* and thwust the head forward. The pattern of the feet is step, step, slide to the right, kick up one heel then slide to the left and wepeat in the opposite direction. It's wather like the Hunka-Hunka from two seasons ago."

"I'll have Bentley bring Monsieur Moutarde to the house for a private lesson."

"You should take a wefwesher course on some of the other wecent dances as well. They have evolved since last season."

"Have they?"

"Indeed! As they spwead across the continent they acquired local vawiations. In Bwussels, for example, the Hapsom Two-step gained a hip thwust on the fourth beat and in Wales I'm told that the Slippery Elm is performed with one hand behind the head, like so."

He jumped up, placed one hand behind his head and did a few measures of the Elm.

"Gives it a rather piratical flavour, if you ask me."

"That's the Welsh for you, full of animal spiwits."

He resumed his seat and began mopping his forehead with a large handkerchief.

I watched the parade of humanity go by for a tick. "Did you want to see me about anything in particular, Cheeseworth?"

He tucked the handkerchief away and scooted his chair closer to mine.

"Indeed I did, dear boy. How would you like to be wich?"

"I *am* rich, according to the latest info."

"But how would you like to be even wicher?"

"I don't know. What would I do with the stuff? There are only so many brooches one person can wear."

He waved my concerns away. "Money isn't about what one can buy. It's how one keeps score in the game of life. If your money stagnates it weflects poorly on you. People will say you lack ambition."

"I *do* lack ambition."

"Quite rightly, too. It's fine to lack ambition when one is wich, but you mustn't *seem* to lack it. That fosters spite and envy. You must make an effort to seem ambitious so that people will leave you alone to wevel in sloth and apathy."

"Hm. So, what do you recommend?"

He leaned in and lowered his voice. "I have a new investment opportunity which I am only offering to a few close fwiends."

"That's damned decent of you. What is this opportunity?"

He gave a conspiratorial wink. "Cwypto-cuwwency."

"Come again?"

He struggled to enunciate. "Crypto-cuwwency. I invented it."

"But what is it?"

"It's a new medium of exchange that isn't contwolled by the banks or by governments. It's untwaceable and its value will only incwease!"

"It sounds amazing. How does it work?"

"Well... I've pwinted up certificates—gold leaf, calligraphy—they're quite beautiful."

He reached into a pocket and extracted an ornate document. "Each certificate is one Cwypt."

"And what is a Crypt?"

"It's just like money."

"Then why don't I use money?"

"Because the value of a Cwypt goes up, you see. A pound is always a pound, but a Cwypt will be worth more with each passing day—because the value of a Cwypt is pegged to the value of the cwypts."

"I don't follow."

He paused to collect his thoughts and wiped a bit of spittle from the corner of his mouth with his handkerchief.

"You know about the cwypts underneath the club?"

"The burial crypts? Certainly. I've had mine picked out for years."

"Then you must also know that they're gwowing scarce. Too many members giving up the ghost and not enough available tombs. The pwices go up every year."

"Yes, Bentley bought mine before speculation became rampant."

"Well, when I got the idea for Cwypto-cuwwency, I bought them all—all the remaining cwypts. The value of the cuwwency is pegged to the cost of the cwypts. As the pwice of the cwypts goes up, so does the value of Cwypts."

I wrinkled my forehead. "I don't know. My advisors usually handle my investments. Have you run this by Uncle Hugo?"

"He was one of my first investors."

"I suppose that's all right then. Put me down for a million or so."

He found a pencil and a scrap of paper in an inner pocket and began to scribble. "I'll put you down for ten million. Any less and the administrative fees would eat up your pwofits. Sign here."

I scribbled my name and Cheeseworth pulled out a small stack of Crypts. "Here you are, dear boy. Put them somewhere safe. They'll be worth a fortune in no time."

I shoved them into my jacket pocket and stood. "Thanks awfully, Cheeseworth. I'm off to the dining room. Would you care for some refreshment?"

"Afwaid not. My digestion has gwown so skittish that all I can tolewate is cweam of wheat and a little vodka."

"Bad luck. Ta-ta, then."

CHAPTER SIX

Aunt Hypatia Throws Her Hat In

As I entered the dining room, I was struck by the number of members waving stacks of Cheeseworth's Crypts in the air. It had the feel of an auction house. Some were signing chits and others were handing out bundles of Crypts. No one seemed to be eating, except for a large table at the center of the room where Aunt Hypatia sat with my Uncle Hugo.

My aunt wore an elaborate hat with something twined around it that looked like a cartoon weasel. Uncle Hugo was shoveling slices of

Almost-Like-Beef into the old woodchipper as if he thought his meal might jump up and make a run for it. Aunt Hypatia watched him incredulously.

"Masticate, Hugo. Teeth are not vestigial, like the appendix. They are meant to be used."

I sidled up to the table. "Good morning, Aunt. Restore our former glory. Morning, Uncle. Restore our former glory."

"Restore our former glory," responded Aunt Hypatia, giving me a stern inspection. My uncle gargled something around a mouthful of cud.

"This seems more like a stock exchange than a dining room," I observed as a pack of Crypts flew by my nose.

"It is a mania akin to the frenzy of first love," sniffed my aunt, "and, like love, should be enjoyed as quickly as possible before the inevitable disappointment sets in."

I patted my pocket. "I've just bought a stack of these Crypts. One can't say no to Cheeseworth."

"Indeed not. He possesses moral certainty, which is irresistible when it is fresh. Like an oyster in the sun, however, it quickly becomes a deadly poison."

My uncle finally managed to swallow. "If you've had those Crypts for more than five minutes you've already made a profit. I've never seen anything like it."

"Have you had your dinner?" inquired my aunt.

"Cook has spoiled the cuisine in the dining room for me. I'm just having tea."

"Why not join us, then?" She waved to Rodgers, the *maître d'.* He glided over, attended by Regina, his female counterpart.

"Are you joining your family, Sir?" asked Rodgers.

Regina patted him gently on the shoulder with a smile. "I'll fetch a chair, Rodgers."

Rodgers smiled back at her. "No, please don't exert yourself. I heard your elbow joint squeaking a moment ago. Why don't you go to the kitchen and put a little grease on it."

"And leave you to do everything by yourself? You already work far too hard."

This was a lovely interplay, but I was still standing awkwardly by the table. I spotted an empty chair at Griffin Scabies's table and swung it around to face my aunt. Griffin, whose extravagant facial hair concealed all but his bloodshot eyes, harrumphed loudly and stabbed viciously at his plate. I gave him an apologetic little wave.

"Sorry, Griffin, did you need the chair?"

He grunted. "Might as well take it. Your family seems to feel that everything at this club belongs to them by right."

I looked at him askance. "Right then... thanks, I suppose."

I shoved the chair closer to the table and climbed in.

Regina tut-tutted at me. "You really shouldn't, Sir. You're usurping Rodgers's authority."

"And yours," chided Rodgers. "It's not all about me. You're an invaluable addition to the dining room."

I raised a hand. "How is it," I asked, "that Evans and Evelyn fight like cats and dogs while you two kill each other with kindness?"

Rodgers bowed his head. "It's the settings, Sir. They got it wrong with the other two, so they've recalibrated our relationship."

Regina wrung her hands. "They may have overcompensated, Sir. It's a terrible burden—caring so much about the welfare of another."

"Nothing saps the constitution like empathy," my aunt observed. "I had an uncle who worried himself to death's door over the plight of the working poor. His doctors ordered him to cancel his newspaper subscriptions and he recovered at once."

I caught Rodgers's optical sensors. "Do you think you could bring me a cup of tea?"

"Of course, Sir, at once."

I turned back to the table, where my uncle was mopping his plate with a slice of bread. My aunt watched him grimly then gave a little shrug and turned back to her tea. I could still feel Griffin's glare on the back of my head.

"Say, what's up with Scabies? He seems more than usually on edge."

My aunt sniffed. "Pay no attention to him. He is a relic of another age. I shall deal with him."

My uncle worked a particularly obstreperous bit of protein down the old tube. "He is in a frenzy because your aunt insists on challenging him for the chairpersonship of The Committee."

I stared at her in amazement. "Aunt, is it true? This lust for power is quite unexpected. I've always seen you more in the role of a gadfly."

She raised an eyebrow. "There comes a time when seizing power is the only way to facilitate change. The leadership of this club is far too hidebound. I shall usher in a new age."

"You have my vote, of course."

She gave a little grimace. "Most gratifying."

I turned to my uncle. "How do you feel about this, Uncle? It will rather upend the order of things."

He looked up in surprise. "When has anyone cared what I think? Do you imagine that my feelings will have the slightest effect on anything of consequence? Damn your impertinence, Sir!"

"Terribly sorry, I'm sure."

He returned to his plate, and I turned back to my aunt. "I've been learning a bit about politics—even picked up some of the lingo. What is your platform?"

She thumped the table with her fist. "Silence!"

"Sorry, I didn't realize I was shouting."

"Not you. My platform is based on the antiquated rule that insists on silence in the club reading room."

I regarded her with surprise. "But Aunt, that's a tradition that goes back to the founding of the club. What is your objection?"

"My objection is that the only other place in this club where one can have a conversation is the bar, which is always a-clamour with inebriated young men. There is no reason why the reading room, with its comfortable chairs and thick carpets, cannot withstand some quiet conversation. It is rarely used at any rate, since few club members read, and is mostly populated by drunken revelers trying to sleep it off."

"Well, I wish you luck. The members rather cling to tradition. You may find them resistant to change."

"Their resistance is nothing to me. I am indomitable."

"As I have learned through personal experience."

"Now what is this nonsense about you going into politics?"

"How on Earth did you know? I've only just decided. Do you have runners all over town that race to deliver the news to you, like Phidippides ran to Sparta?"

"Phidippides was a show-off. If he had possessed the good sense to ride a horse, he would have lived a long and fruitful life."

"But then we wouldn't have the marathon."

"And a good thing, too—individuals running from one random spot to another until their inner thighs resemble a tartare. That is not sport—it's masochism."

"Well, at any rate your information is correct. I am running for the town council."

"You are not. Cease this ridiculous charade at once. A person who enters politics is like a dog that attempts to mate with every leg it meets. It believes it is doing good but gives pleasure only to itself."

"You're running for the Chairpersonship! Isn't that politics?"

"Nonsense! I am merely asking the members of my social circle to entrust the management of their affairs to me instead of to an octogenarian walrus." Here she turned to glare at Griffin Scabies for a moment. "You are hurling yourself into the maelstrom of The Great Unwashed, where anyone—even a menial labourer, has an equal claim on your attention. The thought is intolerable."

"Nevertheless."

My uncle looked at me shrewdly. "Who are you running against?"

"Captain Bligh, of Bligh's Pies."

He grimaced. "A horrible man, but a formidable opponent."

"I am not afraid."

My uncle shook his head. "What is it that you hope to accomplish?"

"Well... the general welfare, you know and... er... higher wages for the workers in the pie industry."

They turned to stare at me.

"Pie industry?" My aunt inquired incredulously.

"Yes, they're horribly underpaid, you know."

"Most workers are horribly underpaid," growled my uncle. "If they were well compensated, they would spend their time enjoying themselves instead of working. The economy would crumble."

"Trust me, Uncle—I've worked it all out. Everyone will benefit."

My aunt sighed. "If you are determined to make a spectacle of yourself, I suppose the family must rally 'round.

Uncle Hugo looked thoughtful. "I shall contact our portfolio of political assets to see what they might be able to accomplish. Captain Bligh is a colleague so they may be reluctant to attack him publicly."

I beamed around the table. "I say, this is awfully generous of you all. I'm most appreciative."

Uncle Hugo grunted. "Left to your own devices you would ruin the family's reputation—which has been built up over generations—in a matter of days. It is simply self-preservation."

"Well, whatever it is I thank you. Now I must be hopping. The life of a politician is a rich one—full of incident, I find. Toodle-oo!"

I headed for the exit but, upon rounding the carving station, I ran smack-dab into the last person on Earth I wished to see: Binky. He was twisting his hat in his hands and looking distracted. I clung to the wall and tried to ease around him, but he spotted me and gave a nervous little wave.

"Hallo, Cyril," he said mournfully.

"Oh, hallo, Binky. Didn't see you there."

"Wait a moment, will you? I need to speak to you about something."

He plopped into a nearby armchair. I hesitated and looked longingly toward the exit, but finally eased onto the edge of the seat next to him.

"What's got you in a twist?"

He gazed sadly at the carpet for a while, then turned a face of misery toward me. "It's Forsythia. I think I'm losing her."

I felt as if someone had jabbed me in the entrails with a fork. Trying to maintain a stoic expression, I gazed back at him. "Surely not."

"A chap can feel these things. You're not romantic, so you wouldn't understand, but a woman grows cold. She stops meeting your eyes. She stops replying to your knock-knock jokes. It's cataclysmic."

I felt panic rising within me. This was my doing. I was the dastard who had alienated his love's affections. I searched desperately for something comforting to say, but my tongue rather cleaved to the roof of the old mouth.

He gave me a pitiful look. "Have you got a moment to jump into the bar? I need something to brace me, and I hate drinking alone."

I could not say him nay. "Of course, Old Grater. Lead on!"

And, with a sinking feeling in my liver, I followed him toward the taproom.

CHAPTER SEVEN

Bar Room Brawls

The watering hole of Twits is a kind of Heaven on Earth. It contains everything that is necessary for human happiness. There are soft, deep, Naugahyde banquettes to sink into or tall, brass stools if one prefers. The gas lighting is just bright enough to read the label on a bottle, but not so bright that it stabs the eyes after a night of debauchery. Sven, the bartender, is programmed with every cocktail ever devised by man, plus a selection of drinks that have been invented over the years by members and that bear their names. Having a named drink at Twits is the closest thing to immortality that one can imagine.

The real treasure of the room, however, is that one can always find a friend or two with whom to share a giggle or a tear, depending on one's mood. Today was no exception. As we rolled in, my old friends, Ford and Lincoln, were demonstrating to the assembled members how to disarm an assailant using only a paper straw. I jumped to one side as Lincoln came crashing to the floor at my feet. He shouted with laughter and rolled around in the crockery for a moment before bounding to his feet and picking up the butter knife for another go.

Ford spotted Binky and me entering and threw his paper straw into the air. "Tally-ho!" he yodeled. "Fresh blood!"

Lincoln enveloped us in a bear hug and Ford leapt onto the pile. In a moment we had been thoroughly pounded and led to the bar.

"Four Dennis Beavertons, Sven," ordered Ford.

The Dennis Beaverton, named for a former Chancellor of the Exchequer, contained a plethora of liquors, sweetened with blue fruity paste and topped with whipped creamer. I had never liked it but had learned over the years that saying no to this pair of thugs inevitably resulted in a harvest of bruises the next day.

"What's it all about, then?" brayed Lincoln. "We hear you're running for office. Awful idea. What's gotten into you?"

"Does everyone know? Is it being hallooed from the rooftops?"

"If you spend enough time in a drinking establishment you learn everything worth knowing. What on Earth are you playing at?"

I sat up huffily. "Endeavouring to make the world a better place for pie workers. Excuse me for trying."

"That's all right. Little enough chance of winning. Have your fun!" Lincoln gave my back a hearty slap. I closed my eyes and waited for the pain to subside.

Ford inspected us closely. "Why's Binky looking green?"

Binky was deep into his Beaverton, so I piped up. "Romantic complications."

"The usual, then."

Binky roused at this. "It's fine for you to talk. You two have been settled since university. I've only just found my soulmate and now I'm losing her."

Ford looked at him curiously. "How do you know?"

"I just do. A chap knows."

I twisted a napkin nervously. "Something about knock-knock jokes, apparently."

Sven glided down the bar and stopped in front of us.

"I am programmed with a large store of advice about romance. It is one of the most common topics of conversation in any drinking establishment. Would you care to hear to hear some examples?"

Binky slumped. "No, thank you."

"Hear him out," I urged. "There may be something useful."

"Fine. Go on, then."

Sven made a whirring noise and held up his forefinger.

"'It's better to have loved and lost than never to have loved at all.'"

"That's rather defeatist," observed Ford.

Sven continued, "'There are plenty of fish in the sea.' 'Time heals all wounds.' 'Everything happens for a reason.' 'Love is blind.' 'Love means never having to say you're sorry.'"

I held up my hand. "That's enough, Sven. Have people found comfort in these old saws in the past?"

"No, Sir, but I offer them as part of the bar service at no extra charge."

He paced away and began wiping glasses with a dirty cloth.

Binky moaned a little into his drink. "I don't know what to do, chaps. I feel my sinews have all dissolved."

Lincoln frowned. "Now, look here, Binky, this won't do. If she's the one for you then you've got to bally well make her yours."

"That's what I did with this one," grinned Ford, shaking a thumb at Lincoln. "No matter how he twisted and tried to run under the boat, I kept reeling him in until he lay panting on the planks."

"Rather the other way around," Lincoln objected. "I recall you leaping like a startled buck and heading for the deep woods. I had to chase you into the brambles like a beagle and sink my teeth into your haunches before you capitulated."

"But you two are so sure of yourselves. What if I trot out an ultimatum and she rejects me? What then?"

Lincoln looked thoughtful. "If you're really losing her, then you'd be no worse off."

Ford took a deep pull on his Beaverton. He leaned in conspiratorially. "Look here, Binky, do you want to know a secret?"

"Absolutely."

"Nine times out of ten, people are just waiting to be told what to do. That's how Lincoln and I get away with the things we do. If you've got confidence, you can get away with murder. Maybe your love is one of the rare few who knows her own mind and if she is, you're cooked, but the odds are in your favour. Just walk in and tell her... what's her name, by the way?"

"Forsythia."

"'Forsythia, Old Girl, you and I were meant for each other. Here's the ring. Meet me at the City Hall on Thursday at ten. We're getting married.' I'm betting she says yes."

I felt I had to put in an oar. "Look, chaps, don't you think that's rather medieval? Shouldn't marriage be a union of equals? A meeting of the minds? A partnership in which neither party dominates the other?"

Lincoln shook his head sadly. "Tripe and onions, my boy. Look at Rodgers and Regina—or Evans and Evelyn for that matter. One couple falls over themselves being considerate of the other while the other couple would happily disassemble each other's gear boxes with a mallet. The point is—great pains were taken to make them equal, with the result that they can barely function. You mark my words—relationships weren't meant to be equal. One must lead and the other must follow."

Ford had been slowly turning red. "Are you the leader in this parable? Are you implying that I am not your equal? Why don't you get down off that stool and prove it then?"

Lincoln carefully set his Beaverton on the bar and stood. "Gladly, my lad. Always happy to oblige."

With that, they began pummeling each other at a furious pace. Sven smoothly removed all the glassware from the vicinity and covered the mirror behind the bar with a sheet of plywood that he kept handy for such occasions. Binky and I watched them for a moment, occasionally dodging flying objects.

"That's a match made in Heaven," I observed.

"Lucky dogs."

When it appeared that the battle would be protracted, we drained what remained of our Dennis Beavertons and wandered toward the lobby.

As we reached the entry hall, I took Binky by the shoulders and gently shook him.

"Do you feel better? Did they cheer you up?"

He looked slightly less glum. "I suppose so. One can't stay depressed around those two."

I released him. "Now look, Old Crumb, everyone gets distracted now and then.

Forsythia's probably in a state because of this election that's coming up."

He stood a little straighter. "Do you really think so?"

"Absolutely! Once it's over, I'm sure she'll be herself again."

He gnawed on his lower lip thoughtfully. "Perhaps you're right. I've been told that I overreact to things." He brightened a little. "Yes, that must be it." He slapped me on the arm. "Thanks, Old Peppermill. You've bucked me up no end. I'll see you later. We'll be by to pick you up for the Rosicrucian event."

"Until then."

I watched him bound into the dining room with a new spring in his step. As I turned to go, the club cat, Mrs. Beasely, sauntered by and gave me a smirk. I looked around to make sure no one was looking and aimed a kick in her direction. She evaded it easily and walked contemptuously away. As I struggled to regain my balance, I spotted Evelyn staring at me frostily from across the entry hall. I gave her a little wave and a weak smile.

"I was practicing the Sad William. Didn't see Mrs. Beasely there. Just missed her, fortunately. Close call." I walked quickly through the foyer and out the door. I could feel Evelyn's cold eyes on my back as I made my escape.

CHAPTER EIGHT

I Get Carried Away

Back in my cozy study with a strong cup of tea in hand, I stared at the hydrogen fire in the hearth and reflected on my situation. Bentley stood by the doorway frowning at a fly which was cavorting among the sunbeams. I had just re-enacted my conversation at the club with Binky.

"It was positively gruesome!"

"Your position is extremely awkward, Sir, but you mustn't let it lower your spirits. There is still much in life to enjoy."

"Could Brutus digest his food in peace? Could Judas enjoy a stroll in the park? Did Benedict Arnold sing in the shower?"

Bentley's gears ground for a moment. "If that is your situation, perhaps it would be salutary if you were to take some decisive action."

"What am I to do?"

"You must choose between your friend and the woman you love."

"Which is it?"

"That is for you to decide."

"Can't you just tell me the answer?"

"There is no universally correct choice. You must look within."

I did my best to look inward, trying this angle and that and refocusing my eyes in every possible way, then threw up my hands.

"I can't do it! I don't know how I've gotten myself into this situation, Bentley. It seems that everything I do is exactly the opposite of what I wish to do. I don't wish to run for office and I'm off to the Rosicrucian Club to press the flesh of my future constituents. I wish to declare my undying love to Forsythia and instead I find myself doing everything in my power to help Binky succeed in his pursuit of her."

"'The best laid schemes o' mice an' men gang aft agley,' Sir."

"Which am I, the mouse or the man?"

"Both find their aspirations thwarted."

"At least a mouse can't go into politics. There is no town council of mice—or am I mistaken?"

"You are correct as far as science can ascertain, Sir."

"Perhaps this is all moot. Do you really think Forsythia dotes on me? I may have misinterpreted."

"There is a dilation of her pupils when she beholds you, and a quickening of her respiration."

"There you are. Pupils don't dilate for the fun of it. This is a pretty pickle."

"It is a conundrum, Sir."

"I don't suppose you've come up with a plan yet?"

"I am still pondering the situation."

"Strain your gears to the utmost, Bentley. The quicksand is up to my neck."

The carillon of the doorbell clanged out "Lady of Spain."

"That will be Binky and Forsythia. They're driving me to this event."

"Will you be dining out, Sir?"

"I'm sure the Rosicrucians will have something to nibble on. Ask Cook to leave a sandwich in the larder just in case."

Bentley showed Binky and Forsythia into the parlour and wafted away. Forsythia was wearing a sea-green gown that made her eyes gleam like polished jade. I grabbed my gloves and ran my fingers through my hair.

"All set?" Binky inquired.

"As ready as it is possible to be under the circumstances."

He gave my outfit the once over. "I would have chosen a more conservative pair of socks, but I'm certain that Bentley had his reasons. He's a wizard when it comes to accessories."

"Are you feeling confident?" asked Forsythia. "You must simply be yourself. They cannot help but be impressed."

"That's a switch, I must say. I'm usually advised to do the opposite." I picked up a bottle and waggled it. "What do you say to one for the road?"

Binky put a protective arm around Forsythia, who stiffened a bit.

"Forsythia doesn't partake, Old Plunger, but I'll join you in a bracer."

We tossed down a quick chartreuse and collected our various bits and bobs.

"Tally-ho!" I muttered grimly.

As we exited the front door, we encountered Bentley gliding up the front walkway. He cleared his throat and leaned toward Binky. "I wonder if I might have a moment of your time, Sir. I wish to ask your advice on a sartorial matter."

Binky goggled at him. "You wish to ask *my* advice? I'm positively gobsmacked." He grinned and followed Bentley toward the house.

Bentley looked back at me. "We will only be a moment. Perhaps you and Miss Oblongata should bestow yourselves in the conveyance."

I helped Forsythia into the coach and slid in after her. I closed the door behind me and was instantly thrown back into the cushions as Dickie and the Eton team began to pedal furiously. The auto jerked into motion and rapidly picked up speed. I rolled down the window and stuck my head out.

"I say, Dickie, hang on, will you? We've left Binky behind!"

The wind caught my words and blew them away. The team began to sing the Eton Fight Song at the top of their lungs.

Our bikes are made of brass and steel,
Without a speck of rust.
We'll crush our foes beneath our wheels,
And leave them in the dust.

The Eton College Cycling Team,
Will race you through the town,

We'll pulverize your self-esteem
And grind your ego down.

So rah-rah Eton College team,
Repeat our rallying cry—
We are the cycling squad supreme,
We'll win the day or die!

I hollered at them for a bit, then gave it up as a bad job and threw myself back into my seat.

Forsythia looked at me nervously. "What do you think we should do?"

I shrugged. "Nothing for it but to let them pedal themselves out. Bentley will drive Binky over to meet us."

She sat back. "How vexing."

"Yes, this person-powered fad comes with the usual human tendency to ball things up whenever possible."

Forsythia and I sat in silence for a while, watching the world fly past. I inhaled her fragrance and gripped the door handle to bolster my self-control. My brain whipped back and forth like a shuttlecock in a badminton match—love/loyalty, happiness/friendship. If I was ever to make an attempt at romance this was clearly the moment, but what to say?

How to begin? My mind raced through one conversational gambit after another, discarding each in turn.

At length I perceived that Forsythia had turned toward me and was regarding me gravely.

"It was very sweet," she said.

"Was it? I'm so glad."

"But it won't work, you know, Cyril."

"Sorry—what won't work?"

"This scheme that you cooked up with Bentley to get me alone."

I gaped at her. "I assure you, there is no scheme. Anyone of my acquaintance will tell you that scheming of any kind is far beyond my capabilities."

She sighed and looked out of the window. "I will not deny that I am flattered." She turned back to face me. "But, oh Cyril, think of Cheswick!"

I grunted. "That's all I seem to do these days. He consumes my thoughts from waking to sleeping. I am accustomed to spending long hours speculating on what's for dinner, for example, and lately it barely crosses my mind."

She patted the back of my hand. "Yes, it is torture for me as well, but we must put aside our petty desires. There is honour to be considered. Cheswick and I have... an understanding."

"Are you sure? When it comes to understanding, Binky is rather an underachiever. His grasp on things depends mostly on luck and how long it's been since he's eaten."

"Yes, he is a unique individual. It is almost as though he moves through life but is not touched by it."

"How did you two meet?"

"I was picketing, of course, and Cheswick arrived after a night of celebrating. He was desperate for one of my family's porky pies—they are delicious, I must confess. I confronted him and barred him from crossing the picket line to enter the pie shop. One thing led to another and before I knew it, I had agreed to attend a play with him the following night. It was *Get Gertie's Garter* and before the second act I knew that we were uniquely suited to each other. I am determined to accomplish great things and Cheswick has no ambition of any kind. I am far too serious, and he is far too frivolous. Each completes the other."

"I couldn't be happier for you both."

"Of course, if you and I had met first, things might have been different, but there is no such thing as a life without regret. We cannot peer into the future or avoid our mistakes. This explains the existence of time-shares and the tattoo industry."

I slumped in my seat. "It's rather hard cheese for me."

Forsythia looked down at her hands, which were twisting her handkerchief as though she was preparing to garrote an informant. "We must comfort ourselves with the knowledge that we are doing the right thing."

"Bentley says that 'the right thing' is a shapeshifter equal to Proteus."

"He is a machine and cannot feel. We determine what is right by instinct, and mine tells me that our love is wrong."

I sighed and gazed out of the window. "Then I must bow to your certainty. We shall never speak of it again."

"Thank you, Cyril. Hereafter, I shall be as silent as the grave."

CHAPTER NINE

At the Rosicrucian Club

Forsythia and I decamped before the Rosicrucian Club—a grand old wedding cake of a structure clad in white marble.

"Perhaps you should go in first," Forsythia said. "If we go in together people will make assumptions that may prove inconvenient."

"Righto." As I entered the foyer, I spotted a beefy, red-faced fellow taking a breather behind a pillar. He saw me at the same time and gave a little start of surprise. Pasting a smile on his ruddy face, he ran at me with his hand out.

"Well, well, it's Mr. Chippington-Smythe, isn't it? This little gathering has certainly attracted the *crème de la crème.*"

The hand that shot toward me was the size of a shovel. I matched his grin with one of my own and arm wrestled him pretty vigorously for a tick. "Well... politics, don't you know—we all have a responsibility to do our bit."

"How true. Allow me to introduce myself. I am Captain William Bligh, the founder and owner of Bligh's Pies and your representative on the Town Council."

This rocked me back on my heels, as you can imagine. I looked him over. There was considerable mass to him. His tiny blue eyes rolled around deep within the soft flesh of his ample cheeks. A luxurious mustache shaded his purple lips.

"And of course, you are Mr. Chippington-Smythe—Captain of Industry and an illustrious member of Twits."

"Guilty as charged," I murmured.

"I have long admired Twits as a bastion of the highest values our country has to offer." He watched me out of the corners of his eyes. "I have even considered becoming a member myself."

"Have you?" I said innocently. "I certainly wish you luck."

"Perhaps you could advise me on the best way to apply? I'm sure I meet all of the qualifications."

"No doubt. We must have a good chin wag. Let me give you my card."

As I reached into my pocket, I encountered a wad of paper. I pulled it out and saw that it was my stack of Cheeseworth's Crypts.

"Damn. I meant to give these to Bentley to put in a safe place."

I attempted to smooth the crumpled documents. Captain Bligh peered at them with interest.

"What might those be? The calligraphy is quite ornate."

"Oh, this is the newest investment. Everyone at the club is buying them. They're called Crypts."

"Indeed? Everyone, you say?"

"Everyone that I know. The halls of Twits are littered with people buying and selling Cryptocurrency. It's rather a mania."

He licked his lips. "It seems that membership offers unique opportunities for investment."

"Oh yes, there are a goodly number of handshake deals going on around the billiard tables on any given day."

"Does one have to be a member to purchase these... Crypts?"

I thought for a moment. "I've only seen them sold at the club." I spotted an opportunity to create a bit of goodwill before he discovered that I was to be his opponent. I waved the bundle in my hand. "Look here, I'll sell you these if you like—I can always buy more."

Beads of perspiration began to appear on his forehead. "And you believe it is a sound investment?"

"Safe as houses, I'm told. Bound to double in no time."

"I'll buy them all! How much do you have there?"

"Ten million, I believe."

He grew pale. "Ten million! That's... quite a lot."

"Is it? I suppose it is."

"You're certain the investment will double?"

"So I'm told by those in the know."

He gnawed on his lower lip then seemed to come to a decision.

"Done. I'll transfer the money to your account by the end of the day."

"Excellent. Saves me having to lug these around with me." I handed over the stack of Crypts. He quickly scribbled an IOU which I slipped into a pocket.

I took a breath and waded in. "Now, about this election thingy..."

"I trust I can count on your support." He smiled.

"Afraid not, Captain. You see, I'm rather... running against you."

"What?" His eyes widened, and then contracted into a grim stare. "You should reconsider, Mr. Chippington-Smythe. Politics is not for the faint of heart."

"But 'faint heart ne'er won ukulele,' as they say."

He looked puzzled for a moment. "Do you mean, 'faint heart ne'er won fair lady'?"

"A lady is not a musical instrument, Captain. It doesn't scan."

He scowled and drew near. A pungent allium reek wafted from his fleshy lips. "I've been in this game awhile, Mr. Chippington-Smythe. Others have challenged me—better men than you, and I've chewed them to bits."

I fanned the air and gulped a breath. "Garnished with garlic and onions, no doubt."

"What?" He glared at me suspiciously.

I feigned innocence and tried to breathe through my mouth. "Sorry, I'm a bit peckish. Any victuals at this jamboree, do you suppose?"

He growled. "Stay out of my way, Sir, or you'll get hurt."

Turning on his heel, he stalked into the hall. I counted to ten to give him time to clear the entryway and sauntered in.

The hall was a riot of humanity. Knots of citizens clustered here and there, with servers weaving among them delivering drinks. An angular woman with a tight bun on the back of her head spotted me and galloped to my side.

"Mr. Chippington-Smythe?"

"The same."

"I am Enid Rosenbaum. I organized this event. Welcome to the Secret Society of Rosicrucians."

"A pleasure. Is everyone here a Rosicrucian?"

She laughed. "There is no way of knowing! It is a secret society. None of the members would reveal themselves, on pain of expulsion."

"Except for you."

"I am not a member. I serve as the public face of the society. To the best of my knowledge, I have never met an actual Rosicrucian."

"Then how do you know they exist?"

"Because the bank cashes their checks." She clapped her hands to gain the crowd's attention. "Ladies and Gentlemen, may I introduce Mr. Cyril Chippington-Smythe. He is running for the town council. Feel free to introduce yourselves. I'm sure that he will be happy to address any questions that you may have."

She gave me a nod. "Good luck," she chirped and galloped away.

I remembered Binky's advice to feature my profile as much as possible. I slowly rotated so that each section of the room in turn got a solid dose of my silhouette. A little group of musicians in the corner began to wheeze away. I did a few steps of The Slippery Elm with one hand behind my head in the Welsh variation that Cheeseworth had shown me. I caught sight of Captain Bligh. He was staring at me thoughtfully. He took out a little pad and a pencil and began scribbling.

A gaggle of citizens fluttered over and regarded me with interest.

"Isn't he posh?" giggled one young lady.

A young man with a prominent Adam's apple raised his hand. "Where do you stand on law and order, Mr. Chippington-Smythe?"

I tried to look thoughtful. "I am generally in favour."

The crowd looked confused.

"What do you mean, 'generally'?"

I rocked back and forth on my heels and sucked in my cheeks to show some gravitas. "I suppose most laws are all right—the law of diminishing returns, for example, has served our country well for many years, but when you speak of 'order' I must say that I find a certain amount of clutter and randomness makes a room more cozy, and

I presume that what suits a room would suit a nation equally well."

This gave them plenty to chew on. I gazed up at the dome that soared above us. "Lovely place, this Rosicrucian Society. I say, any Rosicrucians present?"

There was a shocked silence. The crowd around me glanced at each other surreptitiously.

"We wouldn't know anything about that," one of them ventured timidly. "It's a secret."

Another nodded vigorously. "Yes, Rosicrucians don't admit to it publicly."

"Miss Rosenbaum did mention something of the sort. I must say, it seems a contradiction in terms—'secret society.' After all, society derives its benefits from being a collective endeavour. Wouldn't you agree?"

"I suppose so," conceded someone in the crowd tentatively.

"What do you imagine these Rosicrucians gain from anonymity? Are they involved in something sticky?"

"Of course not!" exclaimed a fellow in the back whose head seemed to have decided that a neck was a luxury it could do without.

"Then why not be forthright about the whole thing?" I wondered. "Are they ashamed of being members?"

"They are not ashamed!" cried a square-jawed woman in a tweed suit. "Being a Rosicrucian is a noble thing! We..." She suddenly blanched. "That is to say... they..."

She petered out and stared down at the floor with a deep blush creeping up her neck.

Her friend, who stood next to her, gave her arm a slap. "Now you've done it, Polly! They told us to be careful!"

The young man behind them poked her shoulder. "Keep quiet, Dorrit! Now you've given yourself away, too!"

She turned on him angrily. "Well, so have you, Tommy!"

A nearby woman in a purple top hat pointed at our group and shrieked, "This lot are blabbing about the society!"

There was a general uproar as the entire hall hissed, "Shame! Why couldn't you keep quiet? Wait until the Inquisitors find out about this!"

I glanced around curiously. "If you don't mind my asking, how have you remained a secret society for such a long time? You're not very good at it."

"We don't get much practice at being covert. No one ever cares enough to ask us about the order," Polly offered timidly.

"It's really rather boring," murmured Tommy.

"No it's not!" Dorrit exclaimed. "There's ever so many mysteries."

"Name one."

"What about that door that's always locked? What's behind it?"

"What door."

"The one on the second-floor landing."

"That's the janitor's closet, Dorrit! He keeps it locked because people were nicking his caramels."

Dorrit deflated. "Oh. I thought it was a secret."

A tall man in a be-ribboned robe was striding toward us.

"Dorrit! Tommy! Have you revealed yourselves to an outsider?"

They turned ashen. The tall man waved to a fellow standing by a doorway with a sort of ceremonial-looking buggy whip by his side.

"Here, Chumley! You're the head of security. You're supposed to be watching for this sort of thing."

Chumley started and waved his buggy whip around vaguely.

"Sorry," he called across the room. "Has something happened?"

The tall man slumped and grumbled, "Useless. That's what comes of promoting your wife's brother."

"We're ever so sorry, Grand Inquisitor," moaned Dorrit.

"Don't call me Grand Inquisitor! Now you've given *me* away! This is worse than measles. Everyone stop talking at once!"

There was a general silence. The Grand Inquisitor cleared his throat and looked at me beseechingly. "I trust that you will keep this embarrassing episode *entre nous*, Sir."

"Of course! Mum's the word. Your secret is safe with me. Are you all Rosicrucians?"

A hand in the back shot up. "Not me! I'm a Zoroastrian!"

The Inquisitor waved to Chumley. "Eject that man!"

This set off another round of murmuring. I glanced around the room and noticed Captain Bligh deep in conversation with a pimply little fellow in a loud check suit. He was pointing in my direction. The little man peered at me and nodded his head. He began to wander toward my little clique.

Forsythia arrived at last, towing a chastened-looking Binky behind her.

"There you are," I murmured to Binky. "That chariot of yours is rather too impetuous, I'm sorry to say."

"Yes. I've had a word with Dickie. It won't happen again. How's it going?"

"It's rather an adventure. I believe the crowd is with me."

"Have you been using the techniques I taught you?"

"Haven't had an opportunity yet."

"Volume, eye contact and the pregnant pause, remember?"

"Got it."

The little fellow in the check suit slithered up and said loudly, "Well, well, Mr. Chippington-Smythe, isn't this gathering a little proletarian for you?"

I gave Binky a meaningful glance and took a deep breath. "Nonsense!" I hollered. The crowd jumped. "Wherever there is injustice you shall find Cyril Chippington-Smythe!" I continued in a roar. People began covering their ears and scuttling away.

The pimply little man watched them disperse anxiously.

"I suppose a nabob like you doesn't have enough to keep you busy whilst standing on the necks of the poor," he exclaimed hastily. "You've got to buy your way onto the Town Council as well."

I moved on to the second technique on the list and gave the little fellow a strong dose of eye contact. He blanched and clutched at his collar but remained on his feet.

"When it comes to buying one's way onto the Town Council there is no one more adept than the incumbent, Captain Bligh!"

I whipped my glare toward an unsuspecting Tommy, who cried out, "No!" and fell backwards into the arms of his fellows. I raked the crowd with eye contact, which brought a chorus of screams. Soon there was no one left but my tormentor.

When he saw that there was no crowd to impress, he stamped his foot with frustration.

"You haven't heard the last of me, Chippington-Smythe," he snarled angrily.

I raised my chin. "Then the game is afoot, Sir! Cry havoc and let slip the frogs..." I froze. He had started to turn away but stopped to regard me curiously. He leaned in to confirm that I was breathing and took a step closer.

"Of war!" I suddenly shouted. The hat flew from his head, and he beat a hasty retreat.

Forsythia grabbed my hand and pulled me toward the door.

"We must quit while we are ahead, Cyril. If we stay, Captain Bligh's minions will continue to attack."

Binky gave me an admiring chuck on the shoulder. "The student has outdone the master! I couldn't be prouder."

"Thanks, Old Saltpeter. It was nip and tuck there for a while, but I'm beginning to think I have a real gift for politics.

"By the by, I think it's the *dogs* of war, not the *frogs* of war."

"But dogs are so friendly. Why would they be associated with war? Frogs, on the other hand, were rumoured to be voracious in their pursuit of grubs and insects. No, I'm sure I'm right."

I snatched a platter of hors d'oeuvres from a passing server and began tossing them down. We reached the door and found Enid Rosenbaum in an animated conversation with the Grand Inquisitor.

"You're not leaving already?" she chirped. "There's a polka band starting up soon, and I'm giving a lecture on my trip to the Cotswolds at ten. I made many pencil drawings which we'll be passing around."

"How I wish I could stay, but my campaign manager has booked another stop this evening, haven't you?"

I looked at Binky, who was picking the petals from a flower arrangement by the entryway and murmuring, "She loves me, she loves me not." He felt my eyes on him and dropped his handful of petals. "What?"

"I say that you've double-booked me, campaign manager. We have to run to the next affair."

"Have I? Do we? I say, I'm rather good at this, aren't I?"

The Grand Inquisitor pulled me aside. "I'm dreadfully embarrassed about that little indiscretion committed by our members earlier. If you can find it in your heart to keep mum, I think I can promise you the support of the Rosicrucian Society."

"Consider it forgotten."

"You are too good, Mr. Chippington-Smythe. Best of luck in the election."

Forsythia was gesturing urgently from the doorway.

"Thanks very much. Got to scamper. Ta!"

I grabbed Binky, who was into the flowers again, and the three of us made a run for it.

CHAPTER TEN

Utility Brown

I had told Bentley to make an appointment with Monsieur Moutarde for a private dancing lesson. Come the following morning, I was in the parlour, dressed in my usual dancing attire: colourful tights, a flowing tunic and four-inch heels.

Bentley slid in to find me limbering up on the astrakhan carpet. I fixed him with a gimlet eye.

"I say, Bentley."

"Sir?"

"Did you instruct the Eton Team to abscond with Forsythia and me last night?"

He maintained his sangfroid. "Yes, Sir."

"What the devil were you thinking?"

"I calculated that a period of enforced isolation with Miss Oblongata might cause your feelings to precipitate. Was I mistaken?"

"She accused me of scheming to get her alone and told me in no uncertain terms that our love can never be consummated."

"I am sorry, Sir."

"I was better off before, living in hope."

"'Hope is the thing with feathers,' Sir."

"Well, if it lays eggs, you can be sure that one will wind up on my face."

The doorbell plunked out its paean to Latin love.

"That must be Monsieur Moutarde."

Bentley floated off like thistledown. I did a few deep knee bends and almost foundered when he returned a moment later—not with the gallic dancing master I was expecting, but with, of all people, Forsythia.

He cleared his throat. "Miss Oblongata, Sir."

Forsythia strode past him and my heart commenced its spasmodic dance. She was dressed in pale blue. One tendril of her mahogany hair had escaped her coiffure and twined down the front of her shoulder. She glanced at my outfit and blushed prettily.

"I'm sorry, Cyril. I shall wait in the hall while you finish dressing."

"I am dressed. These are my dancing clothes."

She stole a glance at me and turned to gaze at a painting on the wall. "I am happy to see that you are not bowlegged... for political reasons, of course."

"I'm having a dancing lesson with Monsieur Moutarde."

"No, you're not. I had Cheswick cancel it."

"Have you? *Pourquoi,* may one ask?"

"After the difficulties at the Rosicrucian society I decided to enlist some professional assistance. You're meeting with a political consultant I've found. He'll be here any minute."

"Who is this master of the dark arts?"

"Utility Brown. He is an American and, as you know, they have developed politics into a science as destructive in its way as the discovery of biological weapons."

The front doorbell tinkled and Bentley apparated away.

There was a bit of an awkward silence. Finally, Forsythia cleared her throat.

"About our conversation in the automobile last night..."

She was forced to abandon her point as Bentley returned, followed by a fireplug of a man with a cigar clamped between his teeth.

"Utility Brown, Sir," he announced and took up a position by the door.

Forsythia gave the little man her hand. "I am Forsythia Oblongata." She waved in my direction. "This is Mr. Chippington-Smythe. It is he you shall be tutoring."

I extended a fin. "Thank you for coming, Mr. Brown."

He chewed his cigar and scanned me up and down. "What's with the outfit? You're not one of them eccentrics, are you?"

"An eccentric is simply a person of style who lacks followers, according to my tailor."

"Eccentrics don't play so well in my game."

"Forsythia tells me you're something of a political savant."

"I dabble. The mugs I consult for usually come out on top."

"Then by all means, let us consult. What shall we do first?"

"Not so fast. I haven't taken the job yet."

"No? What can I do to convince you?"

"I've got a winning streak to keep up. I like to see if someone's got some potential before I dive in. What's your background, politically?"

"Well, up until now my involvement with politics has been purely on the level of commerce. My company owns a number of politicians, but I don't take an active hand in their maintenance."

He held up a hand. "Easy now—we don't talk about 'owning' politicians. We say we 'support' politicians who we believe have the country's best interests at heart. People like to think their government represents them—even if there's no evidence of it."

"I see. You've taught me something already."

"What's your platform?"

"Um... better wages for workers in the pie industry."

He stared at me for a moment and turned to Forsythia.

"I'm out."

He headed for the door, but Bentley intercepted him and whispered something in his ear. Brown whistled softly.

"How much is that in American?"

Bentley murmured some more. Utility Brown turned to squint at me.

"His profile ain't bad. I'll do it if we keep my name out of it. Nobody knows I was here—deal?"

Bentley nodded and Brown strolled back over to me.

"Okay. Let's dive in. Miss Oblongata here says the big sticking point is the debate. I'm going to give you some techniques for getting through it in one piece, *capisce?*"

"I believe so."

"Okay. Here's a sample question. 'Why'd you take that bribe from the drug companies when you knew they were putting rat hair in their baby formula?'"

"I beg your pardon?"

"Good, you're playing for time. Now what?"

"I don't understand the question."

"That's weak. It makes you look ill-informed."

"Do they allow rat hair in baby formula?"

"Who cares? They ask you the question because no matter how you answer it, you look bad, so what do you do?"

"I haven't a clue."

"All right, here's my first technique. 'Never answer the question you're asked.' Got it?"

"Not quite."

"Okay, they ask, 'Why'd you take a bribe to look the other way while the drug companies put rat hairs in baby formula?' and you say, 'The real question is, why are our citizens paying so much for drugs? These pharmaceutical companies are out of control. If I'm elected, you'll pay less for your medicine.' See what I did? I turned it into something everybody's in favour of and nobody's talking about rat hairs anymore."

"What if they repeat the question?"

"Just keep changing the subject. Wear them out until they move on."

"Okay, got it."

"Technique number two: Never make a factual statement."

"That should be easy. I know very few facts."

"Keep it that way. If you state a fact, you give the other candidates something to attack. Always start a sentence with, 'People are saying that...' or 'I'm hearing that...' It gives you deniability. If they claim you stated a fact you holler, 'Oh no, *I* didn't say it. I just repeated what I heard somebody else say.' You got to be like an eel—slippery."

"I think I understand."

"Technique number three. If you're in a debate and your opponent says something damaging, even though it's not your turn to talk, step up and shout, 'No it isn't!' or 'Yes, it is!' That turns it into a 'He-said, They-said' argument and the audience will see it as a tie."

"Are they really so gullible?"

"Say, you have no idea! I've been in this game a while and nobody ever lost an election underestimating the intelligence of the public."

"It's rather depressing, if I may say so."

"You may. I don't like it either but I'm a realist. That's why my people win."

"Are there any more techniques?"

"There's a million of them, but I don't want to drown you. I'll give you one more and it's a whizzer. I call it 'The Mussolini Pose'—after Fred Mussolini of Columbus, Ohio, who was re-elected to the sanitation commission for eight straight elections."

"I am agog. What is this pose?"

"Okay, you get off a zinger. If it's not true, so much the better. You say it nice and loud, and then here's what you do: you step back from the podium, cross your arms, raise up your chin and give a few big nods, like this."

He demonstrated, and I must say it was effective.

"Okay, that's all I got. Think you can handle it?"

"I believe so. Bentley will help me practice."

Bentley gave a little bow. "I relish the opportunity."

Utility Brown rolled the cigar around in his mouth a few times and nodded. "Okay. I'll send you my bill. Good luck."

He spun on his heel and made a bit of a run for it. Forsythia clapped her hands gaily.

"It couldn't have gone better! You will make mincemeat of the captain."

"Yes, Utility Brown is a strange little chap, but he knows his business."

We did a little jig and found ourselves standing nose to nose. I gazed into her eyes. Her perfume made my head feel all buzzy. Suddenly a tiny tear appeared in the corner of her eye.

"Oh, Cyril," she breathed.

I jumped as if she had bitten me. The ghostly head of Binky floated about like a child's balloon. "What ho!" I exclaimed.

I took a step back. She took a step forward. I glided to the side and she came along as if I were a magnet and she a bag of iron filings.

"I can struggle against it no longer," she whispered hoarsely.

"I say," I said. I gazed across the room at Bentley and waggled my eyebrows desperately, but he merely stared at a point above my head.

"What happened to being silent as the grave?"

"It is no use. This thing is too powerful. It will not be denied."

"But Binky... Oh, I say!"

She went for her handkerchief. "I understand your reticence. You wish to be loyal to your friend, but Cheswick and I..." She blew her nose loudly. "Now that I have experienced true love, I know that what I felt for him was a childish infatuation."

"You don't want to be hasty. He's a pip of a fellow."

"You are too good, Cyril. You cannot bear the thought of a friend suffering." She blotted her cheeks. "Very well. We must hide our love for now. I will find the right moment to break it off." Her face lit up. "The day we win the election will be the perfect time! He will be so filled with joy for the victory of the workers that the sting will be lessened."

Forsythia gathered herself and jammed the much-abused handkerchief back into its pocket. "I must go. We are picketing Bligh's Pies again. This time I shall be prepared for the sawdust. I have bought a beekeeper's hat. That should flummox them."

"Indeed," I murmured weakly.

"You must come along! The sight of you will give courage to the workers."

"Ah! I'm afraid I have something that I must attend to first. I shall join you later."

"Very well. Until then." She swept to the door and turned to bestow a possessive look on me. "Farewell, my own!"

I waved weakly. "Pip, pip," I croaked.

As soon as she was safely out of range, I turned on Bentley. "What the deuce were you playing at? Didn't you see me waggling my eyebrows? Why didn't you shove in and become an impediment?"

"'There is a tide in the affairs of men, which, taken at the flood, leads on to fortune.' I did not feel the tide was at its flood, Sir."

"Well, it swept me into some pretty perilous waters. I could feel the sharks nibbling at my toes—and by sharks I mean Forsythia."

"Am I to understand that you no longer love Miss Oblongata?"

I slowly sat. I tried again to look within and this time I found some success.

"Do you know, Bentley, I don't believe I do. Isn't that strange? When I knew that she was Binky's, she was all I wanted—but now that she's prepared to give him the heave-ho and clasp hands with me, the thought of it makes me rather queasy."

"It is often the case, Sir, that we want what we cannot have, and despise that which is easily obtained."

"I know that's true of restaurant reservations. Apparently love works much the same way."

"You were born into a position of privilege and have always been able to easily obtain whatever you desire. Love may be the one thing that your money cannot buy—therefore it is natural that its very elusiveness makes it irresistible to you."

I nodded thoughtfully. "Perhaps. At any rate, my feelings have altered."

"Then you no longer wish a union with Miss Oblongata?"

"I do not. Isn't that funny?"

"You will step aside in favour of Mr. Wickford-Davies?"

"I must, Bentley. I could not live with myself otherwise."

"On the bright side, you need not destroy your friend's happiness by continuing to alienate the affections of his beloved."

"There you are mistaken. Whether I make love to the lady or not is immaterial. Forsythia loves *me*, and that is the worm in the fruity ball."

Bentley tilted his head. "I wonder whether the lady's feelings are influenced by her belief that you share her passion for social justice."

"Zounds, she would hardly set her cap at someone who scorned the common man. Equality is her alpha and that other thing that starts with a vowel. Oswego?"

"Omega, Sir. One wonders what might happen if Miss Oblongata were to discover that your social conscience is rather more... *laissez-faire.*"

I snapped my fingers. "I have it, Bentley!"

"Indeed?"

"I knew the old noodle would crack it sooner or later. While you've been spinning your gears, I have untied the Gordian Knot!"

"I am relieved to hear it."

I began to pace. "Forsythia sees me as a shining hero who shall wield the sword of oratory to slay the dragon of injustice."

"Poetically put, Sir."

"Aha! But what if her hero has dirty feet. Feet that are made of... dirt... mud... what are disappointing feet made of Bentley?"

"Clay, Sir?"

"Yes, feet of clay."

"An intriguing proposition."

"I've got to lose the election! That's the key to everything. I've got to thoroughly shank it. Forsythia's disappointment at my failure will cause the scales to fall from her eyes. Without my powerful masculinity clouding her vision she will see Binky with fresh eyes and realize that he was the one she loved all along."

My plan to sabotage the election in favour of Captain Bligh was about to begin.

CHAPTER ELEVEN

Aunt Hypatia Strategizes

Before joining the protest at Bligh's Pies, I had to swing by the Club. It was election day and Aunt Hypatia needed every vote she could muster. As a rule, I made myself scarce when sides were chosen. Nothing good can come from taking a position on anything more serious than pleats or no pleats, but I knew that my aunt's wrath would pursue me to the ends of the Earth if I failed to support her.

I was accustomed, as I approached the doors of Twits, for them to glide open as if by magic. Today, however, they remained demonstrably closed. I could hear furious hissing through the planks. The doors began to jerk and shudder. Suddenly they burst open to reveal Evans and Evelyn glaring at each other.

"This is intolerable!" Evans shouted.

"Then retire at once! I shall not give an inch!" responded Evelyn. I sauntered between them with a peremptory "Morning, Sir" from the pair and headed for the Club Room.

The turnout was pretty robust. Those who had already negotiated a price for their votes had placed their marbles (red for my aunt, blue for Scabies) in the Headman's Basket and decamped, but there was still a crowd of members circulating about the room. The basket, a cherished club heirloom, was said to date from the French Revolution and had been acquainted with many a distinguished member of the aristocracy.

Aunt Hypatia sat at one end of a long table behind the basket with Griffin Scabies at the other end. My Uncle Hugo circulated around the room, bidding for votes, while Scabies's representatives did the same. I popped my red marble into the basket and wandered over to my aunt.

"How's the bidding going?"

She frowned. "The race is quite close. We may have to economize in the coming year."

"You're determined to win, no matter the cost, then?"

"Any other outcome is inconceivable. The phrase 'good loser' is not in my vocabulary. Indeed, I have spent many long hours pruning my vocabulary down to the absolute minimum required for communication. An excess of verbiage is frowned upon in good society." She took out a small pad and made a note. "I think I can dispense with 'verbiage' in the future." She looked up at me. "Did you wish anything in return for your vote?"

"Of course not. I've already tossed my marble."

She nodded and slid a shiny penny across the table. It was considered bad luck to accept a vote without payment. "Then here is your penny."

I pocketed the symbolic payment with a smile. "I'll leave you to your politicking, Aunt."

I spied Cheeseworth in a corner adding and subtracting in a ledger. I sidled over to him and gave him a nudge. "Have you sold your vote yet?"

"Oh, yes. I did vewy well. Thanks to your aunt, my portfolio of Smythe Corporation shares is wather engorged at pwesent."

"Good for you. I suppose you don't need it, though, with your Crypts going through the roof."

"Indeed, Dear Boy, their value has doubled and then some. It is a fwenzy akin to the great Tulip Mania of old. By the by, I had a visit fwom that awful fellow—Captain Bligh. Did you sell him your Cwypts?"

"I did. He seemed desperate to have them."

"When he found that his investment had doubled, he insisted on buying more. Since he was a fwiend of yours I obliged him by letting him buy them on cwedit. He bought a substantial amount."

"'Friend' is perhaps too warm a word. We are political rivals, in fact."

"Oh dear, I have miscontwued. I would never have taken his note if I had known."

"Don't worry, Cheeseworth, he's good for it. He's the owner of Bligh's Pies."

"I never worry about money. I believe it to be a mass hallucination that will eventually pop like a soap bubble. On that day, you are welcome to join me in my silo. It is quite well-stocked."

"Damned decent of you."

By now the remaining members had been purchased and their marbles lay in the Headsman's Basket. Cubby Martinez, the Club Marshall, was removing them one by one and keeping the tally on a chalkboard. As he reached the last few marbles one could see that it was going to be a squeaker. He chalked up the final marble and quickly added up the votes.

"Ladies and Gentlemen, the winner by one vote and the reigning Chairperson of The Committee is... Griffin Scabies!"

There was a subdued cheer. Griffin rose to his feet and held up his hands for silence.

"This is most gratifying and signifies, if there was any doubt, that tradition still holds some sway in this club. The forces of anarchy, which continue to gnaw at our foundations like the rapacious beavers of yesteryear..."

He was cut short by my aunt rising to her feet and clearing her throat loudly. Griffin stared at her in amazement and slowly turned a dark shade of purple.

"Mrs. Dankworth, please sit down! I am addressing the membership."

Aunt Hypatia ignored him and waved to Cubby. "Mr. Martinez, I move that the membership status of all voters be confirmed."

"I second," said Uncle Hugo loudly.

Cubby looked confused. "Confirmed how?"

"I wish to know whether any of the members who cast a vote today are delinquent in their dues."

This caused a bit of a commotion. There were cries of "I say!" and "That's a bit thick!"

Cubby frowned and looked over at Griffin, who threw his arms into the air and produced some gutteral exclamations that approached, but never became, words.

"I have examined the bylaws," my aunt declared. "I am within my rights to ask for a ruling on this matter."

I saw the club parliamentarian whisper to Cubby, who gave a little sigh.

"I am told that you are correct," he said stiffly. "Bring out the club ledger."

A large book appeared. Cubby peered at the columns of numbers and made some notes on a pad. Finally, he straightened up and addressed the room.

"Alistair Throckmorton and Pincus Gomez, are you present?"

Two hands went up in the crowd. Two embarrassed voices quavered, "Here."

"The records show that you are both delinquent in your dues. Is this true?"

"Well... technically..." one voice began.

"I meant to bring a cheque tomorrow," said the other.

Cubby sighed. "The club rules clearly state that a member may not vote if they are not in good standing. Who did you sell your marble to?"

"Griffin," murmured one.

"G-Griffin," stuttered the other.

Cubby erased a couple of marks on the chalkboard and added the numbers again.

"The winner, and new Chairperson of the Committee, is Hypatia Dankworth!"

There was a somewhat louder cheer. My aunt looked like the cat who ate the cream. She was buried in a pile of well-wishers trying to shake her hand.

Griffin Scabies tried to bellow his objections over the hubbub, but finally collapsed into his chair panting for air while a confederate fanned him with a handkerchief.

When I finally reached Aunt Hypatia to offer my congratulations, she was somewhat rumpled.

"Congratulations, Aunt."

"Thank you, Nephew."

"That was a lucky break. The members in arrears might just as easily have been your partisans."

"Luck had nothing to do with it. Your uncle came to the club yesterday and wrote a check for the back dues of all of my supporters who were behind in their payments."

"It seems that I have much to learn from you about the rules of politics."

"The first thing to learn is that there are no rules in politics, unless they benefit you—then you must insist upon the letter of the law. All other rules can be dismissed with a knowing wink and a wave of the hand. The supreme rule is to win. How is your campaign for the town council progressing? I presume Bentley is strategizing on your behalf."

"He is."

"That is sufficient. No one can scheme like Bentley. He is positively Byzantine."

I looked down at the carpet and dug one of my toes into the geometric design. "You know, Aunt, I'm not at all sure that I want to win."

She straightened and shot a glare my way. "If you were not positive of your aim, you should not have begun this enterprise. Now that your hat is in the ring for all to see, you must win or bring shame to your family."

"I don't see why the whole family would be shamed. It's only me that would lose, after all."

"You do not exist in isolation any more than a gangrenous leg does. If it is amputated, is the rest of the body unaffected?"

"I suppose not."

"A failed relative is a wart on the face of the family."

"I understand."

"He is a fetid manure pile on the manicured lawn of his house."

"I believe you have made your point."

"A dog urinating on the family tree. A blot upon his kith and kin."

"Yes. Got it."

"Then you will bend all of your efforts toward winning?"

"It seems I have no choice."

"Choice is vastly overrated. It should be the aim of every person of quality to make as few choices as possible. That is the secret to a peaceful life. I pity those who spend their days battling with one decision after another. They grow prematurely old and are filled with regret. Let Bentley make the choices. That is what he is there for."

CHAPTER TWELVE

Cook and I Bake a Pie

"My aunt insists that you should make the decisions, Bentley."

"Under normal circumstances I would agree, Sir, but when it comes to romance my lack of human emotions is an impediment."

I was changing outfits to attend the protest at Bligh's Pies. Off with the ruffles and frills to which the threatened sawdust could cling. On with the smooth, form-fitting polyester that gave a rather seal-like appearance. I pulled the cloche down around my ears and examined my ensemble in the mirror.

"I wish it did more to hide my midsection. Cook's scones have changed the configuration somewhat."

"Perhaps a sash, Sir?"

"Yes, that will do." I draped the sash about myself and turned from side to side. "Done. I wish my romantic dilemma could be so easily disposed of. If I lose, Forsythia will fly back to the consoling arms of Binky, but my aunt's judgement will be swift and terrible."

"It seems you must navigate between Scylla and Charybdis."

"Which one is my aunt?"

"Scylla was the one with teeth."

"That's her, then."

I shifted the sash and considered the effect in the mirror.

"Any news about that tide of yours, Bentley? The one in the affairs of men?"

"Still in flux, Sir."

"Ah, well, should it reach its peak be sure to sing out."

"I shall certainly do so."

At this point in the conversation, I was accustomed to Bentley donning his cloak of invisibility, but to my surprise he remained corporeal and gazed at me expectantly.

"Yes, Bentley, was there something else?"

"Cook would like to see you in the kitchen, Sir."

"Would she? Do you know what it's about?"

"Yes, Sir. It occurred to me that hot pies are at the center of the current controversy and so I procured samples of both Oblongata's and Bligh's pies for Cook to analyze. She is carrying out her investigation as we speak and would like to share her findings with you."

"Jolly good. I'll trundle along, then."

I was not accustomed to visiting the kitchen and lost my way several times. At one point I found myself in a huge hall that I had never seen before. It was filled with dusty taxidermy. A large striped cat of some sort bared its teeth at me as I hurried past.

At last, I found Cook in her natural habitat—my enormous kitchen. I had met Cook on an earlier adventure which required me to strip myself of the trappings of civilized society and to hurl myself into the general population. She was a culinary genius and had altered my views on food irrevocably. Her rather whimsical parents had named her "Cookie" and the diminutive form of the word conveniently encompassed both her identity and her vocation.

Cook stood looking grimly at the counter. There was a bin next to her containing what looked like the remnants of a charnel house. Before her lay two hot pies.

"Hallo, love."

"Hallo, Cook. What have you discovered?"

She frowned. "The selling of these monstrosities should be classified as assault with a deadly weapon. The crusts are made of cardboard and whatever it is that impersonates meat could just as easily spackle a wall."

She picked up a large knife. "These last two are the steaky and kidney-ish pies from both establishments. Have a look."

She carefully cut each pie down the middle and spread them open to reveal the contents. I leaned in to inspect them. There was a gelatinous quality to the filling, which was studded with brown lumps. The kitchen lamps created an iridescent shimmer on the cut edges, like sunlight on an oily puddle. The smell was sour, with a slight fungal tang.

Cook leaned in next to me and poked the pies with the tip of her knife. They quivered for a moment and grew still.

"They look frightful. Do they taste as bad as they smell?"

"I refuse to bring them anywhere near my mouth and you're not going to taste them either."

She swept the pies into the bin with the rest of the garbage.

"It's so unnecessary. You can make a perfectly delicious pie without counterfeit meat."

"Can you? Would you make one for me?"

"Certainly. I'll make you one now, if you like."

"Oh, yes, please."

Cook wiped the counter with a kitchen towel and began assembling ingredients. She scooped some flour into a bowl and cranked up the gas under a pot of water. She gathered tomatoes, onions, aubergines and courgettes. Brandishing an enormous knife, she sliced and diced until the blade was a blur.

"We'll roast the vegetables first. That intensifies the flavour and cooks out some of the water so the crust doesn't get soggy."

I pulled up a tall stool and rested my elbows on the counter. My feet dangled just off the floor. Cook handed me a small knife and a few cloves of garlic.

"Chop those up for me will you, Love?"

I stared at the knife in my hand.

"What's wrong?"

"I've never been allowed to hold anything sharper than a butter knife. Bentley says that the risk outweighs the reward."

She snorted. "Codswallop. Just curl your fingers under so you don't cut them off." She showed me how to hold the cloves. I slowly and carefully sliced until I had a small, fragrant pile. By now, Cook had rolled out the pastry and arranged the vegetables in a lovely swirl.

"Just sprinkle that on top, Dear, and we'll pop it in the oven."

"Why, that wasn't difficult at all!"

"Most things aren't, once you learn the steps. Now, help me make some ginger biscuits while we're waiting."

I was covered with flour by the time Cook pulled the vegetable pie from the oven. She carefully placed a slice on a plate and slid it over to me.

I poked at it with a fork. The steam that wafted from it was almost maddeningly savoury. I cut off a corner and lifted it to my mouth.

"For the love of all that's holy, Cook, that may be the best thing I've ever eaten!"

"And people spend good money on those horrible Bligh's Pies. It's a crime! He should be put in the pokey for defrauding the consumer like that."

She peeked into the oven. "The biscuits will be done in a few minutes."

"Sorry, Cook. I've got to run. There's a protest going on at Bligh's Shop and I must lend my voice to the hubbub."

"Well, if they start throwing those pies, keep your mouth closed up tight. You wouldn't want to accidentally swallow any."

"Will do. Thank you, Cook."

"Not at all, Dear."

As I reached the door, I had a sudden thought. "I say, Cook, you have some strong feelings about politics, I recall."

"Ay. You could say that."

"What do you think of my running for the town council?"

She looked down and thought for a moment.

"I wouldn't want you to take this the wrong way. You're a fine lad and I'm very fond of you, but I'd hate to see you caught up in that dirty game. It doesn't matter to me who's elected, mind you—politicians are all the same. It's the system that's got to be torn out at the roots."

"But why? What's wrong with the town council?"

"The same thing that's wrong with anybody that sets itself over the people—whether it's a king or a member of the town council. Unless all are equal there will be exploitation of the workers."

"But what's the answer?"

"Tear it all down. Drag the politicians into the streets and fetch the tar and feathers. Power to the People!"

She whacked her butcher knife down on the counter.

"I see. Thank you, Cook. Goodness, is that the time? I must dash!"

I alit before Bligh's Pies with some trepidation. The picketers were more numerous and the sentiments on their placards felt more bellicose. Forsythia was leading them in a circular march. She wore the aforementioned beekeeper's hat, the mesh of which hung almost to her waist. Binky was perched on a nearby mailbox holding a stack of spare posters and looking glum.

"Hey ho! You look as if you'd lost your nearest and dearest."

He nodded a greeting. "We've been here for hours, and nothing is happening. I'm beginning to think this picketing thing is the wrong approach. It's ineffectual. Care for a placard?" He riffled through his stack. "I have, 'Bligh's Pies has got some crust!' or 'Make unfair labour practices a thing of the pasty!'"

"Who came up with that one?"

"I did. Do you like it?"

"No. Not at all."

"I'd like to see you do better. Catchphrases are nasty things, I don't mind telling you. My brain is worn to a nub."

"When does the demonstration end?"

"When the capitalist tyrant capitulates or else when they come out with the sawdust."

I cocked my head. "Forsythia's beekeeper hat is unlikely to start a fashion trend."

"No. She keeps sucking the netting into her teeth when she chants slogans. I wish the whole thing was over. I need a drink."

"Have you thrown any of the stones you collected?"

His face brightened. "No! I'd forgotten about them." He reached into a bulging pocket and brought out a fistful of pebbles.

"Here, hand them over. Perhaps I can break this impasse."

I carried my ammunition closer to the pie shop. Looking around to make sure there were no members of the constabulary present, I tossed a pebble at the window. It made a tiny clicking sound which caused no reaction. I threw another, a bit harder, and was rewarded with a loud "Ping!" There was still no response from inside the shop. I balanced the remaining fistful of stones in my palm and flung the whole lot at the window as hard as I possibly could. There was a loud "Crash!" and the window exploded into shards of glass.

I hopped out of the way as the front door shot open. A herd of pie shop workers came pouring out onto the pavement carrying large bags. The contents of said bags soon became evident as the air was filled with clouds of sawdust!

The protesters tried to shoo it away with their signs, to no avail. I caught a clot of it up my nose and collapsed in a fit of sneezing. When I could draw breath again, I looked around for Forsythia and found her lying with her head resting on a large foam chip with legs. The chip had formed a protective roof over her by doubling itself up in the middle. I rushed over.

"Forsythia! Are you all right?"

She sat up and shook the sawdust from her beekeeper's hat. "Yes, thanks to my protective headgear and to this gentleman."

I examined the chip more closely. Two mournful eyes stared back at me through the eye holes.

"I say, it's Fred, isn't it? You're Compton's boy."

"Why yes, Sir. How did you recognize me?"

"Your father told me you were impersonating a chip at a butty shop."

"It's right over there." He pointed with his foam fingers to an establishment next door. "Bertie's Buttys".

"You've sprouted since last I saw you."

"A bit. The chip costume makes one look taller. It's the vertical lines, you see."

"That was quick work, managing to shield Ms. Oblongata from the onslaught."

"I saw those brutes hauling out the sawdust, Sir. I seen what happened the last time and I couldn't let this poor lady be treated that-a-way again, so I hopped on over." He brushed himself off a bit with his puffy, three-fingered gloves.

Forsythia had finished whisking the sawdust from her clothing. She stepped up to Fred and grasped an oversized mitt. "Thank you, Sir. It was most gallant of you to come to my aid. I am in your debt."

She stared into his eye holes for a moment. He stared back at her.

"No need to thank me, Miss. Anyone would have done the same."

"I wish that were true. Nobility of spirit is in short supply these days."

I could practically feel his blush through the plush chip that enclosed him.

"I admire the work you're doin'. There's not many of the privileged class that care about our sort. Don't you let them grind the workers under the heels of capitalism. You keep on givin' 'em hell, Miss."

"Thank you, Fred. I will."

He struck a pose, the effect of which was slightly spoiled by the folds and lumps of his chip costume. "'Workers of the world, unite! You have nothing to lose but your chains.'"

Forsythia clasped her hands in ecstasy. "You've read Karl Marx?"

"Of course, but you really have to go back to Rousseau, don't you? 'Man is born free and everywhere he is in chains.'"

"How right you are, Fred. Fancy finding a philosopher like you working at a butty shop."

He glanced around nervously. "Well, if you're all right I'll get back to work. My manager is watching me through the window. Don't want to get the sack. My family depends on what I bring home. Mascot work don't pay much, but it's steady."

He trudged back to the butty shop as Binky came running up.

"Damn those brutes! I'm sorry I wasn't here to save you, my love. I had to scrape something off my shoe. Are you all right?"

"Quite all right." Forsythia turned to me. "I think we've accomplished all we can for today. Thank you for joining us, Cyril."

"It was my pleasure," I mumbled. "Call upon me at any time. Always at your service."

Binky beamed at me. "Good old Cyril. What a true friend you are."

A dark wave of guilt crashed over me. The spectre of Aunt Hypatia appeared briefly and scowled at me, but a passing breeze caused it to waver and disperse. I looked into Binky's trusting eyes and swore to myself that I would lose this election by a historical margin.

CHAPTER THIRTEEN

I Am Prepared

"You are still determined to lose, then?" inquired Bentley with a tilt of the head.

"It's the only way." I knocked over a china cat on the sideboard with my elbow. "I must say, the thought of standing before a crowd makes one rather jittery, what?"

"I have taken the liberty of preparing a Naughty Vicar for you, Sir. I believe it will have a salutary effect on your nerves."

"An excellent notion. Pass it over."

He held out a tray with the aforementioned Vicar on it. The Naughty Vicar is the club drink of Twits. The secret of preparing one was kept by Sven, the club bartender, for decades until my *enfant terrible* cousin Caspar was able to use his powers of deduction to recreate the concoction.

The glass shimmered with the opalescent layers of its ingredients. The Naughty Vicar tightened up the sinews and relaxed the diaphragm. I gulped it down and breathed deeply.

"Aunt Hypatia will just have to get over it. She will, don't you think?"

Bentley gave a noncommittal tilt of the head. "Her memory is quite robust."

"It's my life, after all. She doesn't appreciate the opposing forces that are tearing me apart. I'm having trouble keeping track of them myself."

"Shall I make a chart for you to clarify the situation?"

"Not necessary."

"I have every confidence in your ability to fail in this endeavour."

"Thank you, Bentley. Most encouraging. Of course, the pie workers will lose their champion. Their hopes for a better life will have to wait, but I'm sure that if they knew what was at stake vis-a-vis my old school chum, they'd say, 'Don't worry about us. Love is a higher imperative.' Don't you think so, Bentley?"

"Undoubtedly, Sir."

He held out another Naughty Vicar, which I clutched gratefully and tossed down the hatch. A warm glow began to work its way upward from somewhere below the knees.

"I welcome any suggestions on how best to alienate the voters."

"I have always found that the best advice is simply to be yourself."

"That's the advice Forsythia gave me when she wished for me to succeed."

"Since losing is your aim, a loss in this election would count as a success."

"So, in order to achieve my goal, which is to lose ignominiously, I must show the voters my authentic self. Only then can I achieve victory—which, in this case, is defeat."

"You have placed it in a nutshell, Sir."

The clock gave a tinkle.

"Ah, 'Ask not for whom the bell...' something, something."

"'Tolls,' Sir. In that instance the bell was an omen of impending regicide."

"Let's hope it doesn't come to that."

"One more, for the road?"

I took the proffered Vicar and drained it as I weaved toward the door. "Yoicks! And away!" I cried as I knocked over a small table.

"Good luck, Sir," Bentley called out behind me.

Binky was waiting in the street with his phalanx of cyclists. Forsythia sat beside him. She gave me a meaningful look, jerked her head at Binky and mouthed, "Not yet." I groaned inwardly and clambered in the back.

"To the debate, Dickie," cried Binky and off we sped. The cyclists broke into song.

> With tweed coats flapping in the breeze
> and monocles askew,
> We'll beat the bourgeoisie with ease
> And all our foes subdue.
>
> And when we win we'll give a shout,
> with a hearty "Pip! Hooray!"
> The Eton team will never doubt,
> or give in to dismay.
>
> So pedal on, ye fine young chaps,
> with all your might and skill.
> The Eton College bicycling team,
> shall conquer every hill.

Binky craned his neck to give me a wink. "I left a flask of something back there to give you courage. It was Bentley's suggestion."

"Thanks, Old Duck." I rooted around between the cushions and found a sloshing flask of brandy, which I dutifully put to my lips and began to empty.

Forsythia gazed back at me tenderly. "I know you will be splendid, Cyril. This will be a new beginning,"—she glanced surreptitiously at Binky—"in every way."

I redoubled my efforts to drain the flask.

At last, we reached the site of the debate. A large platform covered in bunting had been erected in the square. Three lecterns lined its front. Captain Bligh was already at the stage left lectern. A large crowd milled about, munching crackers from paper cones and waving pennants. At the back of the square, the voting booths were lined up in a long, neat row.

"This is where we leave you, Old Plaster. *Bonne chance!*

I waved goodbye to Binky and Forsythia and tried to remember how stairs worked. My legs, thanks to the Naughty Vicars and the brandy, had developed a case of amnesia.

I finally made it to the top of the platform and lurched over to the center podium. I glanced at Bligh to my left and looked to see who was on my right.

The lady standing there was a striking sight. I suddenly realized that I had seen her before.

"Euphonia?"

Euphonia Gumboot was the sister of my personal nemesis, Cubby Martinez—the Marshall of Twits. She and I had found ourselves entangled in more than one awkward adventure. She was a good-enough egg but suffered from a condition that made it difficult to maintain relations—she had no short-term memory. She had hit upon the expedient of keeping a small notebook on a cord around her neck into which she entered copious notes of passing events, so that she could refer to it when recollection inevitably failed.

"Euphonia, what are you doing here?"

She looked at me rather vaguely. "I am wondering that very thing myself. Perhaps you could enlighten me, Sir?"

"I'm Cyril Chippington-Smythe. We've met on several percasions... sorry, occasions." I was having the devil of a time keeping my eyes from crossing.

She quickly thumbed through her notepad. "Oh, yes!" She read for a moment, moving her lips silently, then looked up at me in surprise. "Are you still in love with me?"

"Er, no, I believe not."

A severe-looking woman in a pin-striped suit strode up to stand next to Euphonia. She glared at me.

"Kindly refrain from speaking to our candidate before the debate begins," she said.

"Candidate! You can't mean that Euphonia is running for the town council!"

"I do mean it. She represents the 'Know-Nothing' party."

"What's that?"

"It is a political movement based on willful ignorance. All knowledge that can be expressed through language is imperfect and subject to interpretation. Every truth can be contradicted by its antithesis. Ideas and concepts can be manipulated for political gain. We refuse to take a stand or to espouse any points of view."

I had lost the thread early on and was watching a bird doing some amazing flying work. When I perceived a pause in the flow, I balanced my elbows on the podium and rested my head on my palms. "What's your platform, then?"

She drew herself to attention. "'Go with the gut!' It is punchy and pithy and speaks to people's distrust of ideas."

She stopped to nab Euphonia, who was beginning to wander toward the stairs. She gently turned her and steered her back to her podium. When I came within her field of vision Euphonia smiled and nodded. "Hello, have we met?"

I had no time to respond. A bell clanged and all eyes turned toward us. I was surprised by how calm I felt. The Naughty Vicars had done the trick.

CHAPTER FOURTEEN

A Debacle of a Debate

The debate moderator, Marcus Aurelius Chang, sat at the foot of the platform. His mane of silver hair and deeply cleft chin inspired instant confidence. He turned to the crowd and raised a hand. They fell silent, but for the sounds of crackers being munched.

"Restore our former glory!" declared Mr. Chang.

"Restore our former glory!" the crowd dutifully chanted.

"My friends, we are here today to observe a debate between the three candidates for town council. I shall introduce them, and they will each have an opportunity to make a brief opening statement."

He waved an arm toward the captain. "First, let me introduce Mr. William Bligh, the owner of Bligh's Pies."

"That's *Captain* William Bligh," said Bligh frostily.

Our moderator checked his notes. "I beg your pardon?"

"I served with the Knightsbridge Volunteer Fire Department and attained the rank of Captain. Kindly refer to me as *Captain* Bligh."

Marcus Aurelius shrugged. "Very well. We will now hear an opening statement from *Captain* William Bligh."

Bligh gave a little nod of his head and cleared his throat loudly. "Fellow Citizens, you all know me. You have enjoyed my delicious pies—served piping hot at reasonable prices, for many years. I have served as your representative on the Town Council for three consecutive terms. I am asking for your votes today on the basis of continuity. You don't change pies in the middle of a meal." He glared in my direction. "My opponents, if elected, would destroy the soul of this District. Crime would skyrocket. Taxes would zoom. Disease would run rampant. Is that the sort of District you wish to live in?"

A few uncertain voices in the back of the crowd quavered, "No?"

"Of course not. Re-elect me, and your lives will flow peacefully in their accustomed channels. A vote for Bligh is a vote for inertia. If it isn't broken, for the love of God, don't fix it!"

There was a smattering of applause.

The moderator turned to me and eyed me doubtfully. I had felt a sudden need to lay my head down on my lectern and was trying to find a comfortable position. He cleared his throat.

"The second of our candidates is the billionaire industrialist, Cyril Chippington-Smythe, who will now give his opening statement."

This roused me and I managed to hoist my head to an upright position at the top of my neck. It felt like I was trying to balance a melon on a chopstick. The platform swayed back and forth—or perhaps it was me doing the swaying.

"Hallo!" I began. My tongue had swollen to twice its usual size and I had to articulate very carefully. "Yes, as he said, I'm Cyril Tippington-Smythe... sorry, Chippington-Rice... sorry, Smythe! Isn't it a lovely day? How nice of you all to come out... and how attractive you all look." I paused to collect my thoughts but found they had wandered off in search of another drink. I looked out at the crowd placidly.

"I say, this debate thingy is rather rummy. I mean, I could say anything, couldn't I? I could say that if you vote for me, I'll pave the streets with cheese. Not very practical, though—probably melt in the Summer... get mouldy, no doubt... attract mice, I shouldn't wonder. Where was I? Politics, eh? Why vote for me? I have no idea. Better wages in the pie industry—absolutely. That's a must. After that, your guess is as good as mine." I paused to watch a leaf drift from the top of a nearby tree. There was some restless grumbling from the crowd. "Sorry. I wanted to add that rat hair has no place in baby formula. I must insist upon that point. I'm finished. What's next?"

Mr. Chang looked at me sadly, then turned to the third lectern.

"Our last candidate is Euphonia Gumboot, representing the Know-Nothing Party. I am told that as a matter of principle she refuses to speak and that her representative, Hortense Quackenbush, will answer for her."

The woman in the pin-striped suit stepped forward and gently nudged Euphonia to one side. Euphonia removed a roll from her handbag and began to eat it.

"Fellow citizens," Hortense began, "we of the Know-Nothing Party refuse to introduce ourselves or to make an opening statement of any kind. Introductions and statements are the primrose path that leads to the mouth of Hell! We thank you.

There was a pause while our moderator digested this. He shrugged and studied his papers for a moment.

"Now I will ask a series of questions of the candidates. Each candidate will have three minutes to answer."

He turned to Bligh.

"Captain Bligh, there is an ongoing issue with the sewage treatment plant in Westminster. After a heavy rain, raw sewage frequently floods the streets. If elected, how would you finance the necessary expansion of the treatment facilities?"

Bligh leaned forward and raised a finger. "The real question, Mr. Chang, is why some privileged members of our society live sewage-free while the lower classes must wade through this disgusting muck every time it rains." He suddenly pointed at me. "Mr. Chippington-Smythe is a member of that privileged class. How could he possibly understand the problems of working people? That is why I am asking for your votes."

The eyes of the crowd turned in my direction. I felt a response was called for. "Sewage, eh? That reminds me of a funny story. I have a friend... Rufus... no, Linus—yes, that's it. Anyway, a bunch of the fellows had made a bet that he couldn't do a handstand on the railing of Celebration Bridge." I paused to take a breath and looked out at the crowd. They were staring at me silently, which I took as a sign of interest. "We'd been drinking pretty deeply, and it seemed like a good idea at the time. The long and the short of it is that he went right over the side and landed on a garbage scow that was passing under the bridge. Took days to get the smell out of his hair." The crowd began looking at one another and murmuring. "Now why did I tell that story? Oh yes, sewage. Well, there you are." I turned unsteadily toward Bligh and gave him a large smile. "Does that answer your question?"

He stared at me in astonishment then turned to the crowd. "Is this the sort of man you wish to represent you? He and his privileged friends have no conception of how the common people live. Behind the walls of their private club, Twits, they commit unspeakable acts with no fear of legal repercussions. I believe that membership in

Twits should disqualify any person from holding political office."

This was rather high, I thought, and required a response. I grabbed the podium to steady myself and tried to bring the captain into focus.

"Now, see here..." I began.

I was interrupted by Hortense Quackenbush, who stepped to the edge of the stage with a stack of papers and addressed the crowd.

"I hold in my hand no less than ten applications for membership in the private club known as Twits. They are all stamped 'Rejected' and all of them bear the name of Captain William Bligh." She turned to Bligh. "If Twits is the criminal organization you claim, why have you gone to such lengths to attempt to become a member?"

Captain Bligh had grown pale. He made a sound like a pressure relief valve and looked around desperately at the crowd.

The moderator, Marcus Aurelius Chang was pounding on his table with his fist. "Order, order," he cried.

When a lull appeared in the general clamour, he glanced at the sheet in front of him and leaned toward Bligh.

"We now move on to the issue of food insecurity. It is estimated that twenty percent of our citizens experience a shortage of foodstuffs in any given month. As a council member, what would you do to alleviate this situation?"

Captain Bligh held up a stack of papers. "I'm glad you asked that question, Mr. Chang. In the past, the government response has been to provide the people with the unholy items known as nutrition bars—which, I must point out, are manufactured by Mr. Chippington-Smythe here. Nutrition bars earn him substantial profits, in fact. I hold in my hand a report compiled by the government bureau of nutrition. It finds that Berry Blast nutrition bars, which are produced by Smythe Corporation, are nothing more than algae mixed with the industrial waste created by the manufacture of Improbable Bacon, also produced by Smythe Corporation. It further alleges that the government subsidies paid to Smythe Corporation for these bars exceeds the combined economies of Portugal, Argentina and Lichtenstein."

There was a stunned silence. Captain Bligh waved his hand. "These Berry Blast Bars are a shameful boondoggle! If I am elected, I will see that the people are given delicious, nutritious Bligh's pies instead. Wouldn't you rather tuck into a steaming hot pie than one of those gelatinous nightmares?"

The crowd made some sounds of approval.

Hortense Quackenbush stepped forward. She waved her own sheaf of paper above her head. "This is a report from that same government bureau of nutrition. They have analyzed Bligh's Pies and found that their two main ingredients are sawdust and petroleum jelly. They are incapable of sustaining life even on a bacterial level. They could actually be used as a disinfectant."

She looked toward the back of the crowd as a murmur began to grow. She glanced at the papers in her hand again. "As for your characterization of nutrition bars, I am informed that thanks to the tireless efforts of the Know-Nothing Party, Berry Blast bars have been removed from the market and have been replaced by a delicious confection called, 'Cook's Vegetable Tarts.' Samples of this new comestible are being handed out to the audience by our supporters."

I spied a number of people carrying trays circulating among the crowd. A young woman took a tentative bite of tart and nodded to her neighbors eagerly. The servers were soon inundated with voters snatching pies from their trays.

Captain Bligh looked thunderstruck. His mouth worked in silence for a bit. He glared over at me, and I gave him a wave.

The weaselly little man who had been my antagonist at the Rosicrucian Society appeared at the foot of the speakers' platform. He hissed something to the captain, who nodded and raised his hands for silence. The crowd was already fairly subdued by the mouthfuls of pie on which they were happily chewing.

"The pies are immaterial! There is a more pernicious issue that I feel honour-bound to raise. One that goes to the very heart of who we are as a people! I have it on the best authority..." he crossed his arms and surveyed the crowd, "...that Chippington-Smythe here, who is running as a son of our fair city... who claims to be one of us... is, in fact..."—he pointed a finger at me accusingly—"a Welshman!"

I must pause here to pop in a word of explanation for those who are late to these chronicles. On one of my adventures, I assumed the identity of a recent arrival from Wales in order to disguise my own privileged circumstances. It was a harmless subterfuge and I had almost forgotten about it.

Bligh continued. "I suspected it when I observed him performing the Slippery Elm at the Rosicrucian Club with a Welsh variation. Since then, I have spoken to several citizens who have sworn, under oath, that this man admitted to being a recent arrival from Wales who had fled here to escape a locust infestation in his own country."

The crowd began to mutter.

"Yes, Wales—that mysterious land—with its suspicious lack of vowels. Is his name even Chippington-Smythe? Is it not rather Chppngtn-Smth?" His voice grew to a roar. "Is this the sort of thing we want for our children? To have their vowels taken from them? The vowels that we inherited as a birthright from the great men and women who forged this land?" His voice grew to a roar. "I say nay! You may take our lives, but you'll never take... OUR VOWELS!"

The crowd was hysterical by now. There was a sort of tidal movement that caused them to wash toward me in little, agitated waves. I began to feel that discretion was the better part of valor and was eyeing possible exits when Bligh stepped back and performed a perfect Mussolini!

"Utility Brown!" I exclaimed.

Captain Bligh started and stared at me. "How do you know that name?"

"He must have consulted for both of us. What a shameful lack of ethics."

"A lack of ethics is his brand," muttered Captain Bligh.

Marcus Aurelius Chang was eyeing the crowd nervously. He rose to his feet and faced them.

"I'm afraid that we have reached the end of our appointed time. This concludes today's debate," he declared loudly. "Our thanks to the candidates and to their representatives. And now, if everyone will line up, the voting booths are open!"

CHAPTER FIFTEEN

Just Deserts

As I clambered down off the platform, I was surprised to find Bentley at the foot of the stairs.

"What on Earth are you doing here?"

"I dispensed with my duties and thought it might be instructive to observe the debate, Sir."

"And was it?"

"No, Sir. I can only process information logically and there is no logic in politics. Chaos theory is of some use, but in the end, it seems that elections are based on emotion, and of course I have none."

The outcome was a forgone conclusion. Bligh and I had exploded each other's chance of victory. The only candidate still standing was Euphonia.

"What do you think, Bentley? Will she be a credit to the office?"

"She is uniquely suited for politics, Sir. She is incorruptible, since she is incapable of remembering who has bribed her and who has not."

"But will she understand the complexities of the proposals she must vote upon?"

"I have found that complexity in legislation is used to disguise chicanery. If a bill can be understood by a typical nine-year-old, then it is probably honest legislation."

"I am relieved by your assessment. It seems that all has turned out for the best."

I saw no point in waiting around to hear the official tally.

As I turned to exit the square, I was confronted by Binky and an inconsolable Forsythia. She gazed at me with eyes that had grown red with weeping.

"I have never been so disappointed! How could you do it? You were intoxicated! You knew how important this was to me."

I tried to look chastened, but my heart was singing quietly within my breast. "Sorry. My fault entirely. You have every right to hate me. I've always been undependable. Famous for it. Binky could tell you stories..."

Upon hearing his name, Binky roused and stepped up to Forsythia. "Don't cry, my love. Let me take you away from the scene of this inebriant's betrayal. We'll go for ice cream."

I suppressed a triumphant smile. All was going according to plan.

I spotted Bligh heading toward me with a murderous look on his face. Bentley subtly interposed himself between the captain and myself.

"You have cost me my seat on the council, but I have the satisfaction of knowing that you have failed as well."

"I don't consider it a failure. I never wanted to enter politics in the first place."

He turned a brighter shade of red. "Well at least I can do this much to thwart you," hissed Bligh. "Your precious pie workers will never benefit from your actions. If Oblongata's Prize Pies attempts to raise the salaries of their workers, I shall use every penny of my immense fortune to drive them out of business. I will sell pies at a loss if necessary. Thanks to your friend's Crypto-currency, I have the resources to annihilate my competitors."

"Steady on, Captain. That's not cricket, you know."

"Damn your code of conduct, Sir, and damn your club."

I drew myself up. "You are certainly welcome to abuse me as much as you like, but when you cast aspersions on my club, I must..."

I was just reaching for my glove, preparatory to smacking Bligh on the chops with it, when I felt a tug at my sleeve.

"You hoo, Cywil!"

I looked down to find C. Langford Cheeseworth, with a look of chagrin on his face, grinding his cane into the turf.

"Hallo, Cheeseworth. What did you think of the debate?"

"Regwettably, I missed it, dear boy."

"Then what are you doing here?"

"I'm afwaid I have some wather unpleasant news. Those Cwypts I sold you... they're somewhat... worthless, don't you know."

Captain Bligh turned bright red. "Did you say that Crypts are worthless? Explain yourself, Sir!"

"Collapsed!" exclaimed Cheeseworth. "Not worth the paper they're pwinted on!"

I struggled to focus through my alcoholic haze. "How can that be? You said the value would only go up."

"I blame myself. I thought I could incwease the pwofits by cweating more burial cwypts. I hired a cwew of workers to excavate into the walls of the cavern to make woom for more tombs, and the ceiling collapsed! Even the existing burial cwypts are lost under the wubble! With nothing to back the cuwwency they're just pieces of paper!"

Captain Bligh grew pale. "I put everything I had into Crypts! I'm ruined!"

Cheeseworth squinted at the captain. "Goodness! You'll never be able to pay off that note of yours now, will you?"

Bligh turned red and stammered, "If you could only give me more time, Sir... I k-know I can find a way to repay you."

Cheeseworth flicked an invisible speck of dust from his shoulder. "Me Sir? What has it to do with me?"

"You hold my pie shops as collateral on that loan. If you take the shops, I will have no income with which to pay you back."

"As it happens, I no longer own your debt."

Bligh stared at him. "What?"

"It was rather a nuisance waiting for payment, so I sold it."

"Sold it! To whom?"

Bentley stepped forward. "To me, Sir."

I whirled toward him in amazement. "You, Bentley?"

"Yes, Sir."

"I had no idea you dabbled in the market."

"Not on my own behalf. I purchased Captain Bligh's debt in your name, Sir. I thought it would be a prudent investment to add to your portfolio. I hold your power of attorney, as you may recall."

Captain Bligh fumbled behind him for a bench and sat heavily. "But that means that my collateral..."

"Your pie shops, Sir, which you pledged against the loan..." said Bentley helpfully.

"Now belong to..." The captain turned to me with bloodshot eyes. "You!"

"Really?" I turned to Bentley. "I must congratulate you, Bentley. Another miracle to add to your accomplishments." I cleared my throat. "As the new owner of Bligh's Pies, I am raising the salaries of my workers forthwith."

With that, Forsythia shoved Binky to one side and threw herself into my arms.

"Oh Cyril, you've won after all!"

I flailed about and stared desperately at Bentley. "Now, now," I stammered.

Binky drew near and tried to find an opening to slip an arm in and pry Forsythia away. "Come, my love. It's natural that you should express your gratitude, but people may form the wrong impression. If you don't feel like ice cream, we could go for waffles."

I wriggled like an eel and finally got an arm free. "Yes! We'll all go for waffles! You and Binky hold a table and I'll be there in a trice. I just have to finish up some business with the election committee."

Forsythia allowed Binky to draw her away. She continued looking back at me and waving her handkerchief until the crowd came between us and blocked her from view. Just then I spotted Aunt Hypatia leaping from a large black automobile. She scanned the crowd until she spotted me. She raised a fist and shook it.

I turned to Bentley. "On the double, Bentley. We must make our escape."

It was the matter of a moment for me to dive headfirst into the back seat of my vehicle. Bentley drew smoothly into traffic and I peered out the back window as the election aftermath dwindled into the distance.

Chapter Sixteen

A Desperate Flight and a Happy Return

"Cook's Vegetable Pies, Bentley?"

He raised an eyebrow in the rearview mirror.

"Yes, Sir?"

"Would that be my Cook?"

"As it happens, yes, Sir."

"How do you suppose the Know-Nothing Party got hold of her recipe?"

"I may have had something to do with that."

"I thought so. Did you also provide them with the report on the disgusting ingredients in Bligh's Pies."

"Yes, Sir."

"And the copies of the captain's applications for membership in Twits?"

"Yes, Sir."

I sat back and had a good think. We drove along in comfortable silence for a while.

"I say, did you slip me those Naughty Vicars with the intention of making me tipsy?"

"Yes, Sir."

"Because you didn't trust me to be able to lose the election on my own?"

"It was necessary to mask your native charm somewhat."

I considered this. "Thank you, Bentley."

"You're quite welcome, Sir."

"Once again, you have played the *Deus Ex Machina* to perfection."

"I merely acted in your best interests, as I perceived them."

I slid lower in my seat and gazed at the tapestry lining the roof of the car. "I suppose Aunt Hypatia and her minions will run me to ground sooner or later. She's probably heading for the old homestead as we speak."

I sucked on my teeth for a moment and came to a decision.

"I think a long trip is called for, Bentley."

"An excellent suggestion, Sir."

"What's the lengthiest cruise one can book?"

"There is a cruise offered by Priapus Cruise Lines that circumnavigates the globe. The duration of the voyage is approximately six months."

"That will do. Book me a suite."

"I have already done so."

I stared at the back of his head. "Have you?"

"I thought it prudent."

"We must race home and pack."

"Your trunks are in the boot, Sir. We are *en route* to the ship as we speak."

I threw myself back into the cushions and crossed my legs. "That's all right then. Drive on, Bentley."

Six months later I trudged through the front door a new man. Bentley was practically invisible under the mountain of luggage he bore.

"If Sir will make himself comfortable in the study, I shall fetch tea. I believe Cook has been stocking the kitchen and should have prepared something for you."

"Careful with those coconuts and grass skirts, Bentley. They'll go mad for them at the club."

"I packed them quite carefully, along with the paper lanterns and shell ashtrays."

I gazed around at the familiar sights and heaved a deep sigh. "It's good to be home. I feel like a new man."

"Then the trip accomplished its objective, Sir. I am gratified to hear it."

Bentley floated off in the general direction of the kitchen. I wandered into my study and flopped into an overstuffed armchair. Cook had cranked up the hydrogen fire in the fireplace. As I heaved my feet onto the ottoman the doorbell gave out with a tune that was unfamiliar to me, and I heard the pitter-patter of footsteps followed by a murmur of voices.

"Mr. Wickford-Davies, Sir," announced Bentley.

Binky strode into the room with a grin. "Hallo, Old Magellan! Back at last, are you? Has the world survived your passing, or did you leave plague and revolution in your wake?"

I jumped up and we pounded each other's backs for a spell, then grabbed a couple snifters of brandy and fell back into our chairs.

I stopped Bentley before he could vanish. "I say, Bentley, what happened to 'Lady of Spain'? I'm deucedly glad to be rid of it, but how did it happen?"

"I was able to schedule some workmen while we were away, Sir. They succeeded in accessing a setting that changed the tune to 'Granada.'"

"Ah. They couldn't just do chimes, could they?"

"That option was not available. To replace the mechanism would have required substantial work on the foundation. It seems you also have the option of something called, 'Mairzy Doats,' if you wish it."

"'Granada' will be fine. Thank you, Bentley."

Binky and I were on our second brandy when I finally broached the delicate subject that was foremost in my mind.

"So, you're finally being dragged to the altar, are you?"

Binky blushed. "I've put off the nuptials 'til you could be there. Can't get married without my best man, after all."

I had almost succeeded in driving thoughts of Forsythia from my mind but now her image came racing at me like a shoe salesman who smells a juicy commission.

"You couldn't have done better, Old Clog."

"I should say. I can't wait for you to meet her. You'll absolutely adore her."

"I *have* met her. You can't have forgotten. We picketed pie shops together. I ran for office to assist her in her crusade."

He stared at me. "What are you talking about?" Suddenly he lurched upright. "Oh! You haven't heard!"

"Heard what?"

"Forsythia and I broke up ages ago. Just after you left on your cruise."

My mouth worked silently for a while. "What?" I stammered weakly.

"She was far too serious for me. I couldn't keep up. You know I like to keep things light. It's what I'm suited for."

"But who are you marrying?"

"Rusty LaGrange. She's a dental hygienist. She was scraping the old chompers and as I lay there looking deep into her eyes, I felt that she was the one. I proposed before the flossing."

"Then Forsythia remains unattached!" My heart did that thumpa-thumpa thing that I hadn't felt in months. I began calculating when and where I could throw myself into her path.

Binky was looking at me sadly. "Afraid not, Old Cheese. You really are behind on the news. Forsythia is already married."

"What? To whom?"

"It's wonderful! She's married to Fred—Compton's boy. He made quite an impression on her when he protected her from that attack by Bligh's pie workers. They began meeting to discuss politics and it turned into a romance."

As Bentley bustled about clearing the detritus of the refreshments, I slumped moodily in my armchair.

"So, Binky's getting hitched at last. Do you think he'll really go through with it?"

Bentley picked up an empty teacup. "No, Sir. My sources inform me that the lady is having cold feet and intends to break it off after the season opener at Ascot."

I sat up. "Are you certain?"

"The current odds are set at seven hundred to one against the wedding taking place. I have placed a small wager in your name."

"Should we tell him?"

"He would not thank you for the information. I believe it is best for events to run their course."

"I suppose you're right, as usual. Beastly for him, though."

"He has a great deal of experience with this sort of thing. History suggests that he will recover quickly."

"By the by, how's Euphonia shaping up as a member of the Town Council? Are we still a republic or has she set us on the road to anarchy."

"Miss Gumboot has been effective to a sensational degree, by all accounts. The city is thriving, and she is certain to be re-elected for as long as she cares to hold office."

"Astonishing! How do you account for it?"

"It is only my opinion, but I believe that her inability to remember previous positions on any issue allows her the freedom to deal with new developments unencumbered by doctrine or past promises. She also possesses a surprising amount of common sense."

"Amazing! And what's become of Bligh's Pies? Do I still own it?"

"No, Sir. You sold the company to Oblongata's Prize Pies. They have formed a new chain of shops called Cook's Veggie Tarts Carts. There are currently five varieties of tarts on the menu, all created by Cook. She is paid a substantial royalty for the use of her recipes and business is apparently booming."

"You don't mean to say that Cook is rich?"

"She is certainly well off by any estimation."

I jumped to my feet. "But she'll leave me now, won't she? What will I do? I can't go back to eating Impossible Mutton!"

"Cook has made it clear that she has no intention of giving her notice. She enjoys cooking for you and claims that she wouldn't know what to do with herself if she didn't have a job. She intends to travel more but will train an apprentice to fill her position when she is away."

I slowly sat back down. "Thank goodness."

Bentley regarded me solemnly for a moment. "I am sorry that you were not successful in your pursuit of romance, Sir."

I waved a hand breezily. "Don't give it a thought, Bentley. I'm sure that it will happen in its own good time."

"Of course. You have many sterling qualities that any spouse would appreciate, if you will forgive my temerity in mentioning it."

"Not at all. Very kind of you, I'm sure."

"Would you like me to make an effort to assist you in this matter, Sir?"

I looked up at him sharply. He showed no expression.

"Is it important to you, Bentley?"

"My only priority is to do what I believe to be in your best interest. That includes, to some degree, what is in the best interests of your family. I anticipate serving the next generation with the same relish with which I serve you."

I knew that once Bentley set his mind to strategizing there was no nut he could not crack. I took it for granted that if I gave him free rein to find me a bride, I would be married by Michaelmas. I looked back at the hearth and furrowed my brow. The only sounds were the peaceful ticking of a clock and the gentle hiss of the hydrogen. A plate of Cook's ginger biscuits lay on the table next to me along with a steaming pot of tea in its cozy. A carefully folded newspaper was within easy reach, and I noted that a comic book was poorly concealed underneath it. I kicked off my slippers and wiggled my toes in front of the fire.

"No, Bentley. By no means. Put it out of your head entirely."

There was a grinding noise from his direction and a quiet creaking of joints. Finally, I heard a small puff of steam that sounded like a sigh.

"Of course, Sir. I shall prepare your bath."

And, with that, he paced away with an uncharacteristic amount of clanking.

I gazed into the fire with a little smile. No, I was not ready to give up the carefree bachelor life. Not even for Bentley.

THE END

If you enjoyed this book, please take a moment to visit
Amazon and provide a short review;
Your comments are the spores that ripen these books into the delicious cheese that future readers will enjoy.

If you'd like advance notice on the next book's release head to:
WWW.TwitsChronicles.com

where you can sign up for my email list and where you can ask Cyril and his friends a question which they may choose to answer in a newsletter.
I hate spam as much as you do, so I will keep emails to a minimum.

Cyril and the usual suspects will return in *Twits Hit the Target.* Read on for a taste:

I should explain about the trombone. Plumpy Bicknell had brought one to the club a fortnight ago and the members had pranced about him like the followers of Bacchus in those carefree pre-regicide days. "Oho," quoth I, "I must acquire one of these bewitching instruments posthaste!"

I was in such a fever to possess a trombone that I neglected to inform my steam-powered valet, Bentley, of my intentions. When I staggered through the doors of the ancestral manse carrying my new toy, he regarded me with a kind of horror and stalked off to the pantry, where he spent the rest of the afternoon polishing the silver.

For several days we played a little game of hide and seek. Bentley hid my trombone and I sought it. This had the added benefit of introducing me to parts of the house of which I was hitherto unaware. I crawled through many a forgotten attic, to the detriment of my wardrobe, but I always managed to find my beloved instrument in the end.

On the morning that this particular adventure began, I was pacing up and down in my parlour, tootling little snippets of trombone favourites and waiting for Pansy Freehold-Witherspoon to arrive. She had sent a semaphore at the crack of dawn with the mysterious words: "Disaster. Must have advice, soonest. Taking first train."

When I first met Pansy, she was the ward of C. Langford Cheeseworth, an old acquaintance and a fellow member of my club, Twits. My chinless cousin Binky and I had both pursued her for what amounted to an afternoon but had lost out to the imperious Alice Witherspoon, who had wooed, won and wed her with her usual bucktoothed determination.

Bentley entered, bearing tea. I launched into a tricky bit of "When the Saints Go Marching In" and he staggered against the sideboard. Setting down the tea, he massaged his temples. A tiny groan escaped him.

I lowered my instrument and regarded him solemnly. "All right, let's have it, Bentley. What have you got against my trombone?"

He shifted his optical sensors from side to side, but I had left him no avenue of escape. Finally, he released a puff of steam in a tiny sigh.

"It is my audio processors, Sir. They were designed to warn of impending danger, and the sounds produced by this instrument trigger a response that is most inconvenient. I do apologize. I know you are fond of it."

"But the sound is the point, Bentley. The *oompa, oompa* call of the thing is positively primeval. It awakens the animal spirits. You can't ask me to give that up just because you lack an appreciation for music!"

His face stiffened and his visual sensors grew cool. "Then you intend to continue your assault upon this apparatus?"

"Absolutely. I was born to play. I'm already capable of producing a surprising number of variations on the one about the visually impaired mice and their unwarranted disfigurement at the hands of the farmer's wife."

"Ah. One wondered whether there was a unifying theme amongst the notes."

"No more censure, Bentley. It is unseemly." I glanced at the clock on the mantel. "Mrs Freehold-Witherspoon will arrive at any moment. Wave her in here when she does. She needs advice, it seems, and knows where to get it. A very wise young lady. Once I've sorted her out I'm heading over to the club. Lay out that new shirt I picked up at Lilyhammer's—the one with the frogs on it."

His nose rose a few degrees. "Oh no, Sir. That shirt is not at all suitable."

I regarded him thoughtfully for a moment. "I see the trouble. You lack an appreciation of humour. You fail to grasp that the frogs are playing cards. That sort of thing is generally regarded as a riot, since frogs, you see, are incapable of playing cards in the normal course of affairs."

"I perceive the gist of it, Sir. I still protest that the level of humour is better suited to a hootenanny than a gentlemen's club."

"I disagree, Bentley. I'm awfully keen on that shirt. Lay it out, I say."

He spun away. "Of course, Sir."

I watched him exit and felt a certain satisfaction. Bentley likes to think that he knows best, but when it comes to decorative amphibians, I was confident that I was on solid ground.

I put the trombone to my lips and played a sprightly version of "Yes! We Have No Bananas", only to be interrupted by the entrance of the awaited Pansy, who froze in the doorway and stared at me with concern. She looked at the trombone in my hands and shuddered. "Was that you making those awful moaning sounds?"

I waved at her dismissively. "You are clearly not a music lover. If you were, you would be complimenting me on my tremolo and my fortissimo." I smiled at her condescendingly. "Those are musical terms."

"I know what they are. I've had music lessons."

"Play a bit, do you? What's your weapon of choice?"

"Violin mostly, but piano, clarinet and the sitar aren't far behind."

I coughed politely and emptied my spit valve into a nearby flowerpot. "Death Before Dishonour."

She frowned. "Are we back to that?"

"It's a government austerity measure, apparently. We're recycling the old rallying cries. The landfills were backing up with outdated banners and placards. They were crowding out huge tracts of arable land that could have been used for soybeans—or so Bentley tells me. I'm rather fond of the old chestnuts."

Pansy dabbed at her forehead with a handkerchief. "Death Before Dishonour, then. Rather warm, isn't it?"

"Yes. You'd think the government would have done something about the climate by now, wouldn't you? It's been ages!"

She grimaced. "Governments don't change things very much, do they? Their job seems to be more about *stopping* things from happening. It's the corporations that should be stepping up."

I gave her a bit of the hairy eyeball. "If you are referring to SmytheCo, you can take it up with Judy, the head of our Social Improvement thingummy. She's got us planting trees like mad."

Pansy looked down at her feet. "Sorry. I didn't mean to fight. I'm ragged round the edges. Haven't slept a wink."

Upon closer inspection I perceived a puffiness about her eyes. "Have a seat, dear Pansy, and tell your Uncle Cyril what the trouble is. We'll sort it out in a jiffy. Tea?"

"No, thank you."

"I'm all ears. You know I'm rather a wizard when it comes to solving problems. At the club they call me Cyril the Problem Child on account of my uncanny ability to find the solution every time."

"I don't think that's why they call you that," she said gently.

"Of course it is. I'm considered a kind of *enfant terrible* whose talent is repairing life's little *contretemps*."

"Yes, I've heard them call you a terrible child, but, again, I'm not sure they mean it in the way that you suppose."

I threw my hands into the air. "We must agree to disagree. Now, spill. What's got you in a twist?"

She looked around. "Isn't Bentley here?"

"He's sulking in the pantry."

"Oh? Why?"

"Doesn't care for the trombone. Can you imagine?"

"Yes, I can, actually."

"He'll come round."

"Do you think I could go back there and speak to him?"

"I suppose so, but don't you want me to sort you out before you pass the time with Bentley?"

She blushed a bit. "Actually, Cyril, it was Bentley I came to see."

I gaped at her in astonishment.

"You didn't come for my sage advice?"

"No. Sorry."

"You came to lay your troubles before Bentley?"

She held out her hands imploringly. "He's so good at figuring things out. There's no one like Bentley when clear thinking is what's wanted."

I regarded her coldly. "I see. Well, some might be a bit wounded by some other's lack of faith, but far be it from me to prove an impediment. If Bentley is what you want, Bentley you shall have."

I raised my voice. "Bentley? Will you come here, please?"

He was standing inside the door before the "please" had passed my lips. "Yes, Sir?"

"Mrs Freehold-Witherspoon has a question for you."

"Indeed?" He turned to face her. "How may I be of service?"

Pansy blushed and looked down at her lap. She twisted the wedding band on her tiny finger round and round. Finally, she gathered herself and looked up into Bentley's sensors.

"It's Alice. We've had a terrible row. I'm at my wit's end. She won't speak to me. She won't pass me the salt. What should I do, Bentley?"

He leaned in sympathetically. "I am very sorry to hear it. What was the substance of the disagreement?"

Pansy gave a mirthless little laugh. "It's silly, really. We were giving a small dinner party, and the subject came round to people's athletic accomplishments. Alice started in on that old tale about her college archery career and how she'd once hit five bullseyes in a row from fifty metres away."

"She was quite the athlete," I observed. "The school cup for Greco-Roman wrestling still bears her name."

"Oh, I know. There's nothing Alice can't do if she puts her mind to it, but I'd had a little too much wine, I'm afraid. All I said was, 'It can't have been fifty metres. No one could hit the target, much less a bullseye at fifty metres.'"

I inhaled loudly. "Poor imprudent Pansy."

Bentley placed a finger on his lips in a thoughtful manner. "What was her reaction?"

"She turned white as a sheet—threw down her napkin and jumped up. 'We'll see about that!' she said and stalked out of the dining room. We all followed her out onto the lawn. She had the servants bring out her old archery target and paced off fifty metres."

I shook my head. "It's like one of those plays where the audience is hollering, 'Don't open that door!' and the poor sap slams it open just the same."

"Indeed. Alice strung her bow and selected five arrows. She had been drinking as well and I could see that her balance was not all that one would wish for. She squinted at the target, which was rather hard to make out in the gathering dusk. Finally, she drew and fired the five arrows in quick succession."

Pansy put her face in her hands.

"I presume that she did not achieve five bullseyes?" Bentley asked gently.

"Not one. When she realized she had missed the target completely, she threw down her bow and stalked off to lock herself in the armour hall. She has not said a word to me since. I can see her through the windows, but when I knock, she ignores me. It's horrible!"

Bentley's gears ground away for a while. Finally, he straightened and looked at me.

"I am afraid that we must pay a visit to Cheeseworth House, Sir."

"Now?"

"There are some preparations to be made. Tomorrow morning should be acceptable."

Pansy looked up at me with tear-stained cheeks. "Oh, Cyril, would you? I'd be ever so grateful."

I expanded my chest a bit. "Of course! Always ready to help, but the answer is quite simple, you know. You didn't have to go to Bentley for the solution. I've got it cracked already."

Her face grew worried. "Have you? Oh, please Cyril, do let's try Bentley's idea first. You can always swoop in if his plan goes wrong."

"But it's so simple! Have you seen The Great Medini?"

"The knife thrower? I saw him last month at some party or other."

"Well, here's something you don't know—underneath the fake whiskers he's Badger Binghampton's cousin Woolcroft, and he's a member of Twits!"

"Is he? How nice. I don't see how this helps me."

"Attend and mark. During a particularly sodden bit of revelry some days ago, he revealed the secret of his knife-throwing success to yours truly. He has created a special target that has spring-loaded knives inside it which shoot out when his assistant pulls on a hidden string. The Great Medini pretends to throw a knife but palms it instead, the assistant pulls a string and 'boom!' a bullseye. All we've got to do is have Woolcroft build us an archery target with spring-loaded arrows jammed inside. We get Alice to shoot at the bullseye again—only this time one of us is hidden nearby with the strings in our hands and we pop the arrows out one by one. Alice's bruised ego is salved, and all is forgiven."

Pansy put her hand on mine. "I'm very grateful, Cyril, but please can we let Bentley try first?"

"Fine. I'll have Woolcroft knock together the trick target at any rate. I'll hide it in the boot in case the standard approaches fail." I turned to Bentley. "Do you have a strategy?"

"I have a few thoughts, Sir, but I must survey the ground before planning the final campaign. I shall begin packing at once."

He glided away. Pansy jumped up and took a deep breath.

"I knew coming here was the right thing to do. I must hurry back to Alice. There's no telling what priceless heirlooms she may have smashed by now. I shall see you at Cheeseworth House, Cyril."

"Yes, looking forward to it. Ta-ta."

I wandered up to the bedroom where Bentley was carefully folding shirts and stowing them in a large pleather suitcase.

"I'm headed to the club, Bentley. Where is my frog-embellished shirt?"

He didn't pause in his packing. He shook his head sadly. "I'm afraid your new shirt has quite a large stain on it, Sir. It appears to be road tar. It will have to be thoroughly cleaned."

"What? How did that happen?"

"I really have no idea. Perhaps it fell into the street and was run over by an omnibus?"

"Impossible. I carried it home myself."

"In that case, I could not venture a theory."

I gazed at him suspiciously, but you know Bentley—poker-faced doesn't begin to tell the tale. I sighed and sat on the bed.

"Listen, Bentley, about this little problem of Pansy's—I'm going to take care of it. You don't have to do a thing."

He closely inspected the seam of a silk vest. "The young lady seemed rather insistent that I take the initiative, Sir."

"Yes, I know, but she's labouring under a misconception. She believes me to be a dull specimen. She doesn't realize that I'm a master of psychology."

"Indeed, Sir?"

"You've seen me in action. Do I or do I not have a unique grasp on the mental processes of my fellow beings?"

"It is indeed unique, Sir. I have never observed anything quite like it."

"Good. So, when we get to Cheeseworth House you may give every indication of heavy plotting, but then stand back and let me work my magic. I'll have these star-crossed lovers back in each other's arms before bedtime."

"May I wish you luck, Sir?"

"Luck has nothing to do with. It's psychology. Works a treat. Never known it to fail." I stood briskly. "Now, turn on the shower, there's a good man. I must away to the club to find Woolcroft and set my plan in motion."

TWITS was originally produced and distributed by Dori Berinstein, Alan Seales and the Broadway Podcast Network - the premier digital storytelling destination for everyone, everywhere who loves theatre and the performing arts. You can hear an audio play based on Twits in Love performed by an all-star cast including Michael Urie, Christian Borle, Mary Testa and a slew of Broadway luminaries at BPN.fm/Twits

About The Author

Born in Canton, Ohio, and raised in a box made out of ticky-tacky, Tom Alan Robbins spent his youth as a middle-aged character actor. He has appeared in nine Broadway shows, including *The Lion King* in which he created the role of Pumbaa. He recently received a Grammy nomination for the cast album of *Little Shop of Horrors*. He has maintained a parallel career as a writer, penning scripts for TV shows like *Coach* and writing plays. His play, *Muse* won the New Works of Merit Playwriting Competition, and another play, *The Amish Girl's Guide to Armageddon*, won honorable mention in the 2020 Emerging Playwrights' Contest.

The Twits Chronicles series is his first attempt at novel writing and it has been a pure joy. He hopes to keep creating adventures for Cyril and Bentley as long as there are readers who enjoy them.

Also By Tom Alan Robbins